The Wrong Man

Book 2 of the *Love Unexpected* series

Delaney Diamond

D1360172

Chapter One

Talia Jackson had been summoned, and she didn't know why. She rarely made the drive from her condo in Atlanta to this sprawling estate north of the city because she hated coming here. Hopefully the visit wouldn't take long. She had a housewarming to attend.

She parked in the circular driveway of Livingstone Manor, the name she'd given to her grandmother's outrageously large home, because house didn't provide a good enough description and even mansion was an inadequate word.

Constructed in Greek Revival style with columns along the front, the manor sat in the middle of a fifteen-acre property that rivaled the grandeur of the governor's mansion. Twenty-five foot tall American Holly trees flanked either side, and during the holidays, her grandmother paid an exorbitant sum to a tree decorating service to have the trees trimmed and topped with a star. The verdant grass of the expansive lawn resembled a tightly-woven carpet, and a team of gardeners ensured it never grew longer than one and a half inches or her grandmother would be livid and there would be hell to pay.

Before getting out of the car, Talia checked her makeup in the rearview mirror and smoothed her long black hair. The cream pants suit might be too formal for a weekend visit elsewhere, but with her grandmother a stickler for appearances, it was imperative she look her best. Taking one last, deep breath in preparation of the meeting, she wiped her clammy hands on a tissue and exited the car.

The butler answered the door, a somber-faced black man dressed in a uniform complete with white gloves. "Hello, Miss Talia. Miss Maybeth is in the parlor." Her heels clicked on the Italian marble floor as she followed him through the grand foyer to where her grandmother waited.

Maybeth Livingstone barely acknowledged Talia's presence, her gaze flicking over Talia's attire and, apparently finding it acceptable, turned her back to her. She paced in front of the window, a phone to her ear and her voice icy and disdainful. Talia sympathized with the person on the other end because the cutting tone was all too familiar.

Maybeth gave the receiver an earful about a mistake they'd made with a package of documents that should have arrived in her Midtown law office but had been delivered to the Florida office instead. Per usual, she spoke so properly her voice carried a hint of a British accent even though she'd been born and raised in Georgia.

She wore a print skirt and light-colored silk blouse that undoubtedly cost an obscene amount of money. The only jewelry on her body were two Harry Winston diamond drop earrings and a rose-gold Patek Philippe watch—one of several she owned. At sixty-plus-years-old, she had the energy of a woman in her twenties and the facial features of a woman in her forties. Her gray hair was elegantly styled in a bob, flipped up at the ends and contrasting beautifully with the inky blue-black color of her skin.

"You and Carter are divorced."

Talia blinked. She hadn't noticed her grandmother had finished the call. Maybeth never beat around the bush, but how could she have possibly known about the divorce? Talia hadn't told her about her most recent failure.

"Don't concern yourself about how I found out," Maybeth said in her imperious tone. She set the phone on the table. "What's disturbing is that you didn't tell me yourself. I don't believe he was the best choice, but he's as good a man as you could possibly find, and you were married for ten years. I expected the marriage to last, Talia. What did you do?"

Talia's chest hitched with pain. *I didn't do anything.*

The systematic tearing down had begun and she lowered her eyes to her lap, blinking back tears she couldn't allow to fall. If she did, her grandmother would rip her apart. Maybeth despised weakness.

"We grew apart. It happens." She hated the meek sound of her voice.

Why could she stand up to everyone but her grandmother? Because she craved her approval, longed for it more than anything else. Maybeth was the only mother she'd ever known, but she couldn't recall her grandmother ever paying her a genuine compliment or celebrating an accomplishment without pointing out the next rung on the ladder to climb.

"What are your plans now?" Maybeth's sharp voice intruded on her thoughts.

"Plans?" Talia lifted her gaze.

"Don't repeat what I say, Talia. It makes you look foolish. Yes, your plans. You've accomplished the goal of senior VP, now what's next? Without a husband and children keeping you back, the sky's the limit. You could run Omega Advertising if you wanted to, but I don't know if you have the drive."

"I-I...um—"

"Stop stuttering and speak up," Maybeth snapped.

Talia took a deep breath. She clenched her trembling fingers together on her lap and tried to imagine sitting in front of someone else— someone less intimidating who didn't make her feel like an insignificant little pea. "The Santorinis are not going to let an outsider run the firm. It's a family business," she explained. Her grandmother knew that but obviously didn't see it as an insurmountable obstacle.

"You impress them enough and they will." Maybeth's eagle-eye gaze narrowed on Talia. She pursed her lips and shook her head as if she saw something that disappointed her. "It's up to you, but you always limit yourself. You haven't lived up to your full potential and I don't know why. Well, I know why. Too much Jackson blood and not enough Livingstone blood. I swear your mother must be rolling over in her grave wondering why you won't do better when she gave her life so you could have yours."

Talia flinched internally at the brutal assessment. Maybeth always made remarks like that, reminding her of why she didn't have a mother.

"She could have been anything she wanted," her grandmother said often. Instead, she'd "fallen in"—again, her grandmother's words—with Talia's father, gotten pregnant, and lost her life during childbirth.

Maybeth sat down on the sofa across from Talia, her back straight like a queen on a throne observing one of her subjects. She picked up a John Grisham hardcover from the table in front of her, flipped it open, and began to read.

"Next time keep me informed," she said to the pages. "I don't like finding out these things second hand."

And with that, Talia was dismissed from the queen's court.

Chapter Two

Drained. That's how Talia felt after interactions with Maybeth. Drained of energy. Drained of life.

She pulled out from the onramp and back onto the highway. She took a deep breath, then another, and kept to the far right lane—the slow lane—while she regrouped.

She practiced her smile and spoke her mantra out loud. "I'm strong, capable, and independent."

Her hands still shook, but slowly her pulse rate returned to normal. She resisted the urge to press the accelerator to the floor, anxious to get to the party where familiar faces and welcoming smiles would be the perfect antidote to the battering her self-esteem had taken.

Thirty minutes later she turned onto the cul-de-sac where her best friend and her husband were having a party to celebrate the move to their new home. She pulled her car as close to the house as she could. She left her suit jacket in the car and strode the short distance to the house, past all the vehicles lining the street.

Welcome.

The white banner with red letters stretched above the doorway of the two-story Neocolonial house nestled between two other homes on the quiet street. Balloons tied to the mailbox marked "Stewart" waved in a gentle breeze and made it easy for guests to find the location of the party.

Inside the house was as busy as an ants' nest with people milling around carrying drinks and plates piled high with food. Several smiled politely at her, and she smiled back but didn't recognize any faces. A little boy zipped by and Talia hopped out of the way. His mother followed close behind, muttering an apology as she tried to catch up to him.

In the living room, gift baskets and boxes wrapped in bright-colored ribbons and pastel paper covered the middle of the floor. Embarrassed she'd only bought a gift card, Talia glanced around to make sure no one saw her drop it on the pile. She'd been so busy juggling projects at work and moving into her new place, she hadn't had had time to shop for a housewarming present. But her friends, Ryan and Shawna Stewart, would understand. Most people preferred gift cards nowadays anyway, didn't they? Then they could get what they really wanted.

At the back of the house, she entered the large kitchen with its pine cabinets and marble countertops. More people hovered in there and food covered almost every visible surface. The tempting aroma of grilled meat, cooked greens, and a host of other food items teased her appetite and made her salivate.

"Hey, you made it!" Yvonne Wallace, Shawna's older sister, walked up holding her two-year-old daughter.

Happy to see a familiar face, Talia smiled in relief. Her gaze took in the little girl sucking her thumb, head nestled against her mother's breasts. How many children did Yvonne have now? Talia had lost count.

The two women embraced.

"This is quite a spread," Talia remarked, looking around.

Yvonne nodded. "They gave up on the idea of finger food and figured they'd feed everyone a real meal."

"This is more than a meal. It's a banquet."

She took a quick peek under covered containers and found chicken prepared at least three ways, barbecued ribs, rice, and different types of casseroles.

"The heavy food's in here," Yvonne explained. "One of Ryan's friends is manning the grill and we should have hotdogs and hamburgers to add soon."

"Did they think they were feeding an army?" Talia turned and spotted a table filled with pies, cakes, and brownies. She couldn't wait to sink her teeth into the offerings, and her stomach grumbled as a reminder that she'd only had a smoothie for breakfast and nothing else all day.

"I know, right." Yvonne shifted her daughter

higher on her hip. "Ryan and Shawna are in the back yard. If you want, I can give you the grand tour of the house before you head out there."

"Let me get something to eat and I'll find you when I'm ready. Thanks."

"If you need anything, holler. I'm supposed to be one of the hostesses, but I've been doing a crappy job." Yvonne laughed to herself and meandered off.

Talia glanced out the wide windows of the French doors. More people stood around chatting and eating in the big yard. A wooden fence followed the perimeter of the property, providing privacy from the neighbors on either side. A burly guy with a beard and apron worked the large stainless steel grill, carefully placing cooked meat into an aluminum pan. William, Yvonne's husband, sat at a table with Ryan and Shawna.

Ryan, a good-looking man with dark hair and intense blue eyes, and Shawna, always with a ready smile on her smooth, brown face, had been married almost three years. They lingered in the honeymoon phase, forever staring at each other with puppy-dog eyes, as if no one else existed in the world but the two of them.

Their twenty-month-old son, Ryker, so named because all the men in his father's family had a name that began with the letter "R," ran around on the neat lawn with a couple of other kids. With his curly hair and light brown skin resembling an even, all-over tan, he represented a blend of both parents' complexions and features.

The most recent addition to their small family

lay cradled in Shawna's arms—ten-month-old Madison, feeding herself from a bottle. She chugged away, all the while staring intently up at her mother, giving the impression she understood what Shawna was saying.

Shawna's ponytail swung from side to side as she laughed and shook her head against whatever Ryan had said, before punching him lightly in the shoulder. He caught her hand and held onto it. Talia smiled—it was impossible not to—but watching them together made her insides twist painfully, a strong reminder of her newly single status.

The deep timbre of a man's laughter in the hall caught her attention, and she knew right away who had arrived. Oddly, her pulse jumped a little at the sound of his voice.

Sure enough, in walked Tomas Molina, six feet two inches of flirtatious male. Wearing a pair of snug fitting jeans on his long legs and a black T-shirt that stretched over his powerful chest, he already had women eyeing him as if they wanted to take a bite out of him instead of the food on their plates. Natural blonde highlights streaked through his brown hair, which always had a slightly disheveled look, giving him the appearance of someone who'd just rolled out of bed. At least today he'd pulled the unruly shoulder length locks into a decent-looking ponytail.

One woman stroked his ripped bicep, and he flexed the muscle for good measure. "*Buenos días,* Tomas," she purred.

He flashed an open, friendly smile. "*Buenos días. ¿Estas bien?*"

"*Sí, gracias.*"

Rolling her eyes, Talia picked up a Styrofoam plate and began to spoon potato salad onto it. The way women fawned all over him disgusted her, and he lapped up the attention like a true narcissist. She heard him exchange pleasantries with a few other guests while she lifted the plastic wrap on another container and added coleslaw to her plate.

From the corner of her eye, she saw Tomas stroll over with a lazy gait. "Well, well, Talia Jackson is here." He peered out the kitchen window at the sky. "No. No pigs are flying." His Spanish-accented voice, low and husky, reminded her of the actor William Levy.

She and Tomas seldom spoke, but whenever they did, he always had something smart alecky to say. She couldn't for the life of her figure out what she'd done to make him pick on her all the time. Probably because he was an arrogant chauvinist and she had no qualms about calling him on it. Fortunately she knew how to dish the witty retorts as well as he did.

"Oh look, *another* T-shirt. What a surprise."

He apparently never met a T-shirt he didn't want to own, and it seemed his entire wardrobe consisted of them in all colors. He wore them so tight they banded around his large biceps and molded to the contours of his muscular chest.

Unfazed, he responded, "You notice what I wear? I'm flattered."

"Don't be," Talia said.

He folded his arms and leaned a hip against

the counter. "I'm surprised you came."

"Why wouldn't I be here for my friends' housewarming party?"

He shrugged. "You're such a busy woman. You hardly ever hang out, and every year Shawna invites you to my picnic on Memorial Day weekend, but you never come."

"If I didn't know better, I'd say you're disappointed I don't." She lifted the aluminum foil on another container, and when she found the baked chicken, she added a leg to her plate. "Tell you what, I'll come this year so you won't feel so neglected."

"I like it better that you don't," he said.

"*Riiight.*" She smirked at him and added corn on the cob to her plate.

She felt his gaze on her, and a prickling sensation crawled up the back of her neck. He had a way of looking at women as if he was undressing them with his eyes. She didn't know if he did it on purpose or not, but it made her feel stripped bare in his presence. Every time he came near, she became hyper-aware of him and a little anxious, a little…breathless. Even his voice made her feel odd. She liked the sound of his rich baritone too much, and the physiological responses she experienced at his proximity were clearly inappropriate.

"We should call a truce," he said.

"Are we at war?"

He chuckled. "You always have an answer, don't you? No, we're not at war. At least, I don't want to be. We should try being friends since our best friends are married to each other."

"That would be boring, wouldn't it, if we got along?"

"So you like fighting with me, is that it?" His eyes mirrored the question. They stood out against his swarthy skin, and she wondered how she'd never noticed how attractive they were before. Light brown. No flecks of green or other colors, only a pure, antiqued gold like a strong whiskey.

Did she like arguing with him? Maybe she did. Their sparring matches always left her buzzing with energy afterward, and after the meeting with her grandmother, she welcomed the interaction.

"Even if I do," she said, "you like it way more than I do. You're always the one who gets the fights started, like you did a minute ago."

"Only because you need it."

"Need it?" Talia cocked an eyebrow. "You have to explain what you mean."

"You're one of those women who can get out of hand, so I have to keep you grounded. You have a...*cómo se dice*? Oh, I remember." He snapped his fingers. "You have a Napoleon complex."

She shot him her *Are-you-for-real?* look. "I don't think so."

"Yes, you do. It's because you're so short." He sliced his hand horizontally from his nose over the top of her head. "See?"

Talia stood up straighter, as if she could grow taller by sheer will power. "I do not have a Napoleon complex, and anyway, I'm pretty sure that only applies to men."

He looked amused. "No, I'm sure the complex

applies to women, too. I have a perfect example standing right in front of me. How's the weather down there?"

She cut her eyes at him and continued searching for food.

"No response? I'm so disappointed," he said.

"I'm ignoring you for the rest of the day."

"This is a first. I silenced Talia Jackson all by myself, and I didn't need to tape her mouth. I should make an announcement." He picked up a piece of baked chicken with his hand.

"*There are tongs.*" Talia held up a set. "What are you, a barbarian?"

"We called a truce, remember?" He bit into the chicken and winked.

She stared at him for a moment and then shook her head, laughing. He was so ridiculous. How freeing it must be to do as you please and not worry about what others think.

She noted the expression on Tomas's face but couldn't decipher the look.

"Why are you looking at me like that?"

He took another bite of chicken and finished chewing before he answered her question. He grinned. "You should smile more."

Chapter Three

Tomas almost laughed out loud at Talia's stunned expression. Priceless.

The ice princess wasn't so icy after all. He'd obviously given her something to think about. With a quirk of his brow he tossed the bone in the trash before grabbing a napkin to wipe his hands. He went out the back door, leaving her behind. She could think about what he'd said while he relaxed outside with Shawna, Ryan, and William.

Greeting his friends, he dragged a chair over to the table to join the conversation.

"I like the new place," he said, dropping into the seat.

"Thanks," Ryan said. "If she'll stop buying stuff, maybe one of these days we'll be settled in and comfortable." He placed a hand on his wife's denim-clad knee.

"Don't listen to him," Shawna said. On her

lap, Madison gnawed her chubby fingers, observing the adults around the table with big brown eyes, uncannily similar to her mother's. A pink headband partially covering her curly black hair matched the pink and white onesie she wore. "Of course I'm going to pick up things to decorate the house, but he's the one with the problem. He's already built a wardrobe for the baby room, but that's not enough. He insists we need to redo the walk-in closet in the master bedroom because he hates those iron thingy shelves, and he wants to replace all the cabinets in the kitchen and bathrooms."

"The craftsmanship just isn't there," Ryan explained. "But other than the storage situation, we love the house."

They all laughed. Ryan made custom furniture and tended to be more critical than the average person about woodwork, but Tomas understood. He often critiqued homes he entered because he built houses.

"I thought Talia would be here by now," Shawna said, looking toward the house.

"She's inside," Tomas said.

"Oh, she's here? I didn't know."

"I don't think she's been here long. She was putting a plate together when I saw her."

Shawna stood and placed a hand on Ryan's shoulder. "I'm going to check on her and see how she's doing. You want anything while I'm inside?"

"What about me?" William spread his arms wide, pretending to look offended but not quite succeeding.

"Aren't you supposed to be putting together the scavenger hunt for the kids?"

William groaned. "I don't know why I let Yvonne talk me into overseeing the hunt. This is my first weekend off from the hospital in weeks, and I still have work to do." He was a doctor at Northside Hospital.

"You better hurry up before she finds out you haven't hidden those items," Shawna warned, the corners of her mouth lifting into a soft smile.

Still muttering to himself, William rose from the table and headed to the house. Shawna raised an inquiring brow at Ryan to get an answer to her question.

"I don't need anything. Thanks, love," he said.

She dropped a kiss on his lips before following William, and Tomas watched Ryan watch her walk across the lawn. When she disappeared into the house, Ryan finally turned his head in Tomas's direction.

"Ryan, you're a lucky man."

He laughed. "Don't I know it."

"So tell me about the job." Tomas worked as a foreman for a residential housing contractor, but he also took side jobs to supplement his income. Ryan had mentioned a possibility earlier on the phone.

Ryan pulled a folded piece of notebook paper from his pocket. "Here's the name of the guy and the address. He wants to knock out a wall between the kitchen and dining room. I went by there to take a look and you could probably complete the job in a couple of weekends. Once you're done with the renovations, I'll install the cabinets."

"Thanks." Tomas tucked the note into his pocket. He could always count on Ryan to send him business. "So what's the deal with Talia?" he asked, trying to sound casual.

"What do you mean?"

"Are she and her husband really having problems?"

"Oh, you haven't heard? They got a divorce. It became final about a month ago."

"You're kidding." Tomas leaned forward. "They were married for what—ten years? That's a long time."

"It didn't work out." Ryan shrugged.

He mulled over this new information. "How old is she? Late twenties, right?"

"Twenty-nine."

That made Tomas four years older than her.

"If I remember correctly," Ryan continued, "Her grandmother introduced her and her husband at some political function during her freshman year in college, and they got married the following year. They work together now, which I bet must be pretty awkward." Ryan sipped his beer. "He's a bit older than her, too—around forty-three, forty-four, something like that."

Tomas stroked his chin. He'd never met the man, only heard about him. The times he'd seen Talia at social gatherings, she'd always been alone. "Do you know him well?"

Ryan shook his head. "Not really. I met him a few times. Shawna knows him better than I do since she and Talia have been friends for a few years."

He'd heard the story of how the two women

met. Talia had gone shopping in Shawna's clothing boutique one day and they'd hit it off.

Tomas glanced back at the house. "Divorced. Huh."

What had happened? Was it the husband's fault? Their split certainly didn't have anything to do with Talia letting herself go. Her makeup was always immaculate, and today her thick hair flowed down her back in black, glossy waves. From the day he'd met her, not once had he ever seen a strand out of place. He wondered fleetingly if it felt as soft as it looked.

She always smelled so damn good, too, and had a queenly bearing which added to the impression of aloofness that surrounded her. Yet she wasn't aloof at all. Quiet would be a better word to describe her personality because she always spoke to anyone who spoke to her, but she never seemed quite comfortable at their social gatherings and tended to stick to the people she knew well.

She had a musical quality to her voice, even when she ripped him a new one. Maybe that's why he couldn't resist harassing her every time he saw her. He wanted to hear that sweet voice. With her catlike eyes and dark umber skin glowing like polished stone, she was easily the most striking woman at the gathering and exuded a confidence that had always made him pay extra attention to her. And those rose-tinted lips—full, puckered. Damn, her ex-husband had been a lucky son of a bitch for ten years.

He intended to ask Ryan another question when his gaze collided with his friend's disapproving blue eyes.

"No," Ryan said.

"No, what?"

"No, you can't date her. No, I won't hook you up because she's one of Shawna's best friends and Shawna would kill me. And no, you can't date her."

"You don't have to say it twice."

"I thought I should repeat it." Ryan sipped his beer again and pinned Tomas with a lethal stare.

"I don't blame you for your reaction, but I'm not a monster," Tomas said dryly. "It's not like I pillage villages and ravish blushing virgins. I tell women my philosophy on dating upfront so there are no misunderstandings."

He had nothing to offer in the way of commitment and most of the women he slept with wanted the same type of arrangement. If they were interested, they were treated to an exciting short-term relationship, and at times his generosity involved sending them on their way with parting gifts. He preferred to live his life without the trappings of monogamy and couldn't understand why Ryan and other men chose to settle down. Shawna was a good woman, but there were so many other women out there to sample.

Black, white, Asian, Latin. Blondes, brunettes, redheads.

Voluptuous, slender.

Introverts, extroverts.

An endless list of possibilities existed. How could a man limit himself to one? The very idea bordered on the ridiculous. Till death do us part went against nature. He was certain of it.

"Normally I'm indifferent to whatever or whomever your latest conquest is," Ryan said. "Personally, I think karma's going to get you one day. But this time, I've got to run interference, buddy. Talia's my wife's best friend, and she's my friend, too."

Tomas understood his friend's need to protect, but still...

"I'm not the Grinch who stole Christmas," he said.

"You're not exactly Santa Claus, either," Ryan countered. "Don't go there."

"If you continue, you're going to hurt my feelings, *amigo*."

"I'm trying to put this into perspective for you and make sure you lead with your top head and not the bottom one."

"I always lead with the top head, but the second one does follow close behind."

Injecting humor into the conversation should have lightened the mood, but Ryan didn't respond to his effort. With a thoughtful frown on his face, his friend twisted the beer can in a circle several times on the tabletop. "Leave this one alone."

"It's not me, it's the women," Tomas said. That was partially true. Women threw themselves at him all the time. Was it so wrong to give them what they wanted? "They love the accent."

"The accent, huh?" Ryan said skeptically. "See if you can turn off the charm. Your love 'em and leave 'em tactics are not a good idea this time around. She hasn't even been divorced two months yet. I would hate to see her get hurt."

"*Coño*, I understand," Tomas said, throwing up his hands. "You want the Big Bad Wolf to stay away from *Caperucita Roja*. I promise not to eat her." He couldn't resist a lascivious smile at the double entendre.

Ryan sighed heavily and shook his head. "You're hopeless. Speaking of eating, have you eaten yet?"

"I had a piece of chicken."

"Come on, then. You have to help us get rid of this food, and make sure you take a plate with you. Hell, take a couple of plates." He stood and patted his stomach. "I think it's about time for round two for me anyway."

"Only round two?" Tomas gave him a good-natured slap on the back. "You're slipping."

They made their way across the lawn, stopping to speak to friends on the way in. Once back in the house, Shawna hurried over.

"I haven't found Talia. Where is she? Have you seen her?" The words rushed out of her mouth and she looked decidedly worried.

Ryan gave his wife his full attention. "What's wrong?"

"Carter's here," Shawna whispered.

Ryan frowned. "What's he doing here? You didn't invite him, did you?"

"Of course not." Shawna gnawed a corner of her bottom lip. "Well, not exactly. When I sent out the invitations two months ago, it went to their house because Talia hadn't moved out yet. He must have assumed he was still invited even though they're divorced now. The thing is," her voice lowered even more, and Tomas strained to hear, "he's not alone. He brought Paula with him."

"He brought his new girlfriend? He's got some nerve." With a hard set to his jaw, Ryan set his plate on the counter. "See if you can find Talia, and I'll get rid of him."

"I last saw him in the living room," Shawna said as Ryan walked away.

Tomas knew he should mind his own business, but he couldn't help but be curious to see the man Talia had been married to for ten years. He followed Ryan to the foyer.

"Hey, Carter, how's it going?" Ryan said to a tall, fair-skinned black male coming out of the living room on the other side of the staircase. A black woman almost as tall as Carter, but who appeared to be about twenty years younger, followed closely behind.

"Ryan, it's good to see you." Carter shook his hand. "Congratulations on the new house."

Then, perhaps the worst thing that could happen, happened. Talia descended the stairs, laughing and talking to Yvonne. When she saw Carter, she stopped and her eyes widened. At the same time, Shawna hurried from the kitchen and screeched to a halt when she observed the catastrophe about to take place. William strolled in the front door, and a group of children raced ahead of him, screaming and giggling and almost knocking over the adults in the entryway.

No one moved. No one made a sound as they waited for Talia to react. And then she did.

She stormed down the stairs and marched

over to Carter and his girlfriend, her body rigid and face contorted in anger.

"How dare you come here? And how could you bring *her*?"

Chapter Four

Polished, educated, Carter Anderson III was the perfect man. Now he had the perfect girlfriend, Paula, beautiful and very tall. Her height felt like an insult, a strike at Talia's diminutive size.

The fact that he hadn't batted an eyelash when she'd asked for a divorce didn't sit well, and Talia's anger had only magnified when he'd arrived at the company picnic a couple of weeks ago with his new girlfriend in tow. Now, for him to show up at the housewarming struck a nerve.

She'd let him have the house and most of the possessions they'd accumulated while together, but these were *her* friends. He had no right to be here and bring another woman. Her nails bit into her palms as she curled her fingers into angry fists.

"Talia, I didn't know you'd be here," Carter said. "If I'd known—"

"How could you not know?" Talia shouted. "Shawna's my best friend!"

"Calm the hell down," Carter said.

Ryan stepped forward. "Guys, this isn't the time or place. Carter, you should go."

"You were seeing her before we got a divorce, weren't you?" Talia asked. The question had haunted her since she'd found out about their relationship. "And you couldn't wait to flaunt your little slut in my face."

"I'm not a slut," Paula said from behind Carter, looking hurt and incredulous.

"She's not a slut, and for the record, I never cheated on you, but I don't think anyone would have blamed me if I had. I should have, because God knows you could push a man into the arms of another woman."

"You are absolutely despicable," Talia said.

"What's the matter, upset because you can't find anyone yourself?" Carter's voice dripped with venom, and the caustic remark cut her to the core.

Guests slowly approached the scene, some peeking around the corner to find out who the raised voices belonged to.

"Who says I don't have someone?" Talia lifted her chin.

"Who would put up with you?" he shot back.

The stinging words constricted her throat, but she swallowed past the pain. "You think *I* was the problem?" she asked, wanting to lash out. Wanting to hurt him. "Maybe it wasn't me. Maybe I had to find the right man; one who could make me happy and *satisfy* me."

She narrowed her eyes and felt a perverse sense of satisfaction when a small gasp erupted from the group. Carter's cheeks darkened to a ruddy hue.

Ryan held up his hands. "Guys, really, this is getting out of hand."

William nodded his agreement. "He's right. Enough already."

"Nice try, Talia," Carter sneered. "You're as cold as a dead fish, and I know you're not seeing anyone."

Cold. She hated that word. She wasn't cold or unfeeling, no matter what he thought. It bothered her that he found it skeptical that she could be seeing someone. As if she couldn't find another man if she wanted to. Because he didn't want her, he thought her undesirable. It hurt but made her angry, too.

"Shows how much you know. I have a man." The lie tumbled out easily, because if Carter could move on, then dammit, so could she.

"Oh really?" Carter mocked, looking around. "What's his name, and where is this mystery man?"

Silence descended on the group, and with all eyes on Talia, she froze. Heat rushed up her neck. Her mind went blank and she couldn't think of a single answer. Within minutes the day had gone from bad to worse. First, chewed out by Maybeth, and now she was about to be embarrassed in front of all these people.

"I'm right here."

Her heart jumped when she heard a deep voice speak up, one she never expected. Like everyone else in the room she swung in the direction of the sound. Tomas came forward, his walk slow and cocky. She barely managed to refrain from hugging him with a rush of gratitude.

He stopped beside her, and as she looked up into his brown eyes, her muscles relaxed and the weight of embarrassment eased from her shoulders.

"That's right," she said, her voice more confident.

She placed a hand on his arm and her heart jolted. She'd never touched him before. He had big man hands and arm muscles so rigid she thought he could crack nuts in the groove of his elbow.

She ignored the shock on the faces of her friends and their guests and relished Carter's dumfounded expression. She couldn't have picked a better replacement than Tomas. Younger, virile, large and muscular, anyone could see the improvement.

"When did this happen?" Carter demanded. His gaze flitted from one to the other.

Tomas moved closer and slipped his arm around her back, plunging deeper into his role in the deception. His hand landed low on her spine. A little too low. So low he grazed the top of her behind. She stiffened at his touch, though at the same time it triggered warm sensations in the lower half of her body and sent her pulse into a riot of movement.

"We don't owe you an explanation," Talia replied, "but it...it just sort of happened."

Residual nerves from the contact with Tomas still shook her, and the inviting smell of him filled her nostrils. Bergamot and lime.

"Yes," Tomas agreed. His eyes mischievous and twinkling, he added, "You could say it...happened out of the blue, no?"

Talia nodded her head vigorously. "Yes, that would be a good way to sum it up."

"You have some nerve talking about me when you've already moved on yourself," Carter said through gritted teeth. His eyes flashed angrily at Talia.

Talia lifted her chin triumphantly. "What did you think? I'd be sitting at home, twiddling my thumbs and pining away for you?"

Carter laughed, an ugly, contemptuous sound. "You know what, Talia, I'd hoped we could take the high road and find a way to get along, but that's simply not possible with you."

She left the semicircle of Tomas's arm. "You don't know anything about the high road," she hissed. "Once I got the job *you* wanted, you couldn't wait to end our marriage because of your insane jealousy."

A muscle in Carter's jaw flexed. "You think I cared about the VP position? The problem with you," he said, jabbing a finger in her face, "is your entire life revolves around success and work. I swear if you could have sex with your job, you would. Our marriage was over long before you got that position. You're heartless and selfish, and this guy better know what he's getting himself into because he's in for a rude awakening."

"Watch your mouth when you're talking to

her," Tomas said, a menacing undertone to his voice. He stepped up beside Talia.

"Trust me, buddy," Carter said, "you're going to regret ever getting involved with her, because all she cares about is her social standing. She's a selfish, inhumane bitch, and she doesn't have a warm bone in her body."

Talia didn't realize she was about to slap Carter until her hand landed across his cheek with a loud crack, leaving red marks on his skin. In the next instant, he lunged at her with pure fury in his eyes, fist raised. She cried out when his hand caught the top of her blouse, but the fabric slipped between his fingers as Tomas pushed her out of the way and grabbed Carter by the neck, slamming him into the wall.

"Have you lost your mind?" Tomas growled into Carter's face.

Talia gaped at the unfolding events in a breathless fog, watching in helpless panic as Carter swung at Tomas, but he dodged the blow.

"Whoa! Whoa!" Ryan jumped between both men and shoved Tomas away. At the same time, William grabbed Carter and twisted one arm behind his back. Both men scuffled until Carter gave in and stopped struggling against William's hold.

Heart hammering, Talia pressed a hand to her throat. Shawna pulled her close with an arm around her shoulder and squeezed. A tremor rattled through Talia at the rage her ex-husband had expressed. She'd never seen him lose control before. They'd had their arguments, yes, but not once had he ever made a move to put his hands on her, no matter how much she pushed his buttons. His reaction chilled her.

"You see what you did, Talia? You have me acting like a maniac," Carter shouted.

"Let's go," William said. "You should have never come here in the first place." He continued to restrain Carter and steered him toward the door. Paula followed, her gaze glued to the floor.

"She'll drive you nuts," Carter yelled over his shoulder to Tomas. "You can't compete with her lifestyle and you'll never be good enough. Good luck. You're going to need it!"

The door shut behind them and an ominous silence settled over the entire entryway. No one moved. The guests were in a state of shock, mouths hung open, eyes stretched wide. A couple of parents had covered the eyes of their kids.

Talia heard Ryan apologize and encourage everyone to go back to what they were doing. Yvonne, who had remained immobilized on the staircase, hurried down and helped him usher everyone in the direction of the kitchen.

"Okay, folks. There's still plenty of food, and we have a wonderful scavenger hunt planned for the kids." Yvonne's cheery voice receded toward the back of the house.

"Are you okay?" Shawna whispered into the quiet.

"I'm fine." Talia couldn't quite look her friend in the eye. She'd ruined the party with a horrible scene, and she was still shaking after the confrontation. "I better go."

"Don't leave. Talia, take a minute—"

"No." She finally looked into Shawna's

worried eyes. "I'm fine. I'm sorry about all this drama. I know how you hate drama."

"Would you stop?" Shawna touched her arm. "You're my friend and I'm worried about you. You shouldn't leave now, when you're so upset."

"I won't feel any better if I stay, and I don't want to talk right now." The adrenaline high was wearing off, leaving her numb and empty. Carter's characterization wounded her deeply. She covered Shawna's hand on her arm and squeezed. "I'll be fine."

"At least let one of the men walk you out in case he's out there."

"He's not going to hurt me."

"You don't know that."

"I do know," Talia insisted. "I was married to him for ten years. That's not Carter. He lost it for a second, but he won't harm me."

"I'll walk her out," Tomas said behind her.

"It's not necessary," Talia said, embarrassed he'd been part of the confrontation between her and Carter. What must he think after hearing all the horrible names her ex-husband had called her? She avoided looking at him.

"I don't mind." The determination in his voice brooked no argument.

"Let him walk you out." Shawna pulled her in for a hug. "Call me. Please. Let me know you're okay," she whispered.

"I will." She hugged Shawna tight, taking comfort in the embrace.

She waved goodbye to Ryan in the hallway and walked out the door. William was coming back up the steps, and she gave him a wan smile before averting her eyes from his look of pity.

All the personal problems between her and Carter had been laid bare for everyone to see. How much he despised her, how far apart they'd grown. Their marriage had started to crumble a few years ago, but the demise had come at an accelerated rate within the past year. She couldn't pinpoint exactly when it happened. She only knew they barely tolerated each other toward the end, like two roommates forced to live together in a too-small house with too many memories. They hadn't made love in over a year and had been sleeping in separate rooms for months before the divorce.

Walking to the car, she heard Tomas's footsteps behind her. She stopped at the driver's door and felt she should say something. She cleared her throat and turned to face him. "You didn't have to volunteer to be my boyfriend."

He hooked his thumbs in the loops of his jeans. "I wanted to."

"I appreciate it, but you got dragged into the middle of my mess."

"I'm a big boy. I can take care of myself."

Her eyes flicked over him. "I see."

"What do you see?" he asked. A smile tugged at the corners of his mouth.

A heated flush climbed up her neck. "You know how to handle yourself in a fight, and...you know...you have big muscles." Very big, and firm to the touch.

"I work out," he said, keeping his eyes pinned on her and obviously enjoying her discomfort. He ran a hand under his shirt, rubbing his stomach. "Not like I used to. I'm getting soft."

Not that Talia could see. She caught a flash of tanned skin and her fingers itched to run over the same area. The skin there appeared to be as firm and smooth as his biceps.

She cleared her throat again. "Well, like I said, thanks."

He tilted his head, analyzing her face. "Are you sure you're all right? Okay enough to drive?" His look of concern made her want to burst into tears. Made her want to be held and told that she wasn't a heartless bitch.

"Never better," she lied. "It's not like I'm drunk." But she would be, once she arrived at her condo. She had a bottle of tequila and margarita mix in the freezer to welcome her home.

He continued to study her, as if he didn't believe her. "It's too bad you're leaving."

"Why? Because you'll miss me?" She needed to joke around, to enjoy the normality of their banter. Their back and forth teasing always made her feel better, and she needed to feel better.

"Miss you? No way. It's just that I won't have anyone to pick on when you're gone."

She pinned on a happy face, falling into the comfort of their repartee. "I'm sure one of those women back there will be happy to oblige you in whatever you want."

"But none of those women are you."

She blinked. The comment took her by surprise. He didn't mean anything by it. Did he?

"Unfortunately for you," she said, keeping the conversation light, "you'll have to make do without me. Don't be too sad. I'll grace you with my presence another day."

"You promise?"

She paused, uncertain. She looked at him, and he looked right back at her. His face didn't give anything away, and she couldn't tell if he was flirting or not. Was he flirting with her?

"I..." For the second time that day, he'd made her speechless. She moistened her dry lips with her tongue. "I...um...I don't make promises often," she finished lamely. She found her keys in her purse and held them up. "Time to get out of here."

"It's okay to turn to your friends," he said quietly.

She froze, staring at her reflection in the driver side window. "Is that what you are? A friend?" She was relieved he stood to the side and couldn't see the light of hope in her eyes.

"I am right now."

And that made her want to cry. What the hell was wrong with her? Tears filled her eyes and she blinked them away in a hurry, fumbling for the door handle. "I'll let you know if I need a friend," she said, her voice husky.

She sat in the car, but Tomas held open the door so she couldn't pull it closed.

Their eyes locked, and she noted the concern there, his eyes searching her face. "You do that," he said.

He shut the door and sauntered away. *Sauntered*, because he never rushed anywhere.

She started the car and waited, not knowing why until he turned at the door and waved. She'd been waiting for him to turn around. Her heart took flight and she waved back, feeling a tad bit silly at how excited she'd become, just because he'd acknowledged her one last time.

Even after he went inside, she didn't drive away but sat there, pondering the events of the day. She'd never thought of Tomas as the sensitive type, but maybe she'd been wrong. First the compliment about her smile, then rescuing her from an embarrassing situation with her ex, the I'm-not-sure-if-he's-flirting-with-me comments, and now what seemed to be sincere concern. She wasn't sure he was the same man she'd spent the past couple of years arguing with whenever they happened to be in the same room.

She didn't know who this new Tomas was, but she was starting to like him.

Chapter Five

The following day, Talia stared unseeing out the window of her tri-level loft. A light drizzle dampened the ground and cloaked the outdoors with an ethereal cloud, making her want to crawl back into bed. Normally she worked every weekend, but today she wanted to get her house in order.

She'd intended to unpack ever since moving out of the house she had shared with Carter and moving here, but she hadn't done much to make this new place feel like home. The walls were bare and boxes filled with her personal effects remained stacked out of the way. A few had been opened to retrieve necessary items, but for the most part they remained untouched.

She reserved most of her energy for work, but it seemed from the minute her feet crossed the threshold each night, she became a listless shell. She couldn't stomach herself anymore.

Today she was turning over a new leaf.

"I'm strong, capable, and independent," she said aloud. Enough with the self-pity.

Upstairs, she changed into a cream blouse, dark brown pumps, and tan slacks. The first item on today's agenda was a trip to the hardware store to purchase paint, brushes, and any other necessary tools for the project she had in mind.

The entire loft was decorated in modern Scandinavian design with neutral colors, mostly white. Today she would add some color.

****

The long line at Home Depot set Tomas's teeth on edge. He preferred to get in early and leave before the rush, but his mother had called from Cuba that morning and delayed his trip to the store. Not that he minded, since he looked forward to their conversations and news from home.

She'd called to thank him for the extra money he'd sent last month, but the conversation lasted over an hour. She went into detail about the birth of his younger brother's first son. He already had three girls, but his brother had celebrated the entire night his son was born, getting drunk and smoking cigars on the porch with his rowdy friends. Tomas wished he could have been there to celebrate. Having not seen his family in years, he longed for the closeness they'd shared. It would be good to see them in the flesh.

The line moved and he stepped forward. Idly, he let his gaze roam, checking out the do-it-yourselfers, when a flash of cream caught his eye. His stomach curled into a knot, and he jerked his head to the right, spotting Talia before she disappeared down the paint aisle pushing a cart.

The debate of whether or not he should say hello lasted all of two seconds before he left the line and followed in the direction she'd gone. He sidestepped a customer who blocked his view, craned his neck, and saw her stop. His pulse spiked to an unnaturally high level, but he controlled his body's outer reaction by lumbering over to where she stood in front of the paint cards.

"Well, well, well," he said, gliding up beside her. "Today must be my lucky day."

Her arched brows lifted in surprise, but once she recovered, a tiny smile—as if she tried to hide it—adorned her lips. "That makes one of us," she said.

"Oof." He grabbed his stomach, as if she'd wounded him. "That hurt."

She giggled, pulling her lower lip between her teeth. What would those lush, soft-looking lips taste like if he ran his tongue across them?

"Whatever," she said. "What are you doing here?"

"Picking up air filters for my lawn mower." He held up the package. "And you?"

"I'm going to paint an accent wall in my living room and one in the kitchen." She ran her fingers over the sample cards in the red and pink family. She had neat, short nails with a clear coat of polish over them.

"You're going to paint?" he asked, surprised.

Talia placed a fist on her hip. "Why do you sound so shocked?"

He raked his gaze over her, from the top of her head—where a tortoiseshell clip held her long hair in a low ponytail—to the pumps on her feet. "You're not dressed like the typical do-it-yourselfer. See the way I'm dressed?" He waved a hand over his paint-spattered T-shirt and jeans. "This is what normal people wear when they work on their houses."

"I'm not working on my house right this minute," she said in a crabby voice, which was oddly attractive. For some reason he couldn't help digging at her every chance he could. "When I get home, I'll change into something more comfortable."

The thought of seeing her change into *something more comfortable* had him conjuring images of skimpy, lace-edged lingerie. She looked like the type to have drawers overflowing with teddies, negligees, and matching bras and panties. He shifted from one foot to the other to ease the ache blossoming in his crotch.

"Have you ever painted before? Do you know what to buy?" he asked.

Uncertainty flitted across her features. "I..."

"I thought so. Let's start at the beginning. What color did you decide on?"

"Um...I like the reds. This one." She pulled a card marked red passion.

He studied her bent head. "You sure you don't need help?"

Her head snapped up. "I want to do this myself." Her voice held a steeliness he hadn't expected, and he admired her determination.

"Okay, then you need the right tools."

"Are you going to tell me what they are or stare at me all day?" She cocked a brow.

Had he been staring? He did a mental headshake. "All right, Miss Personality. Come this way."

He spent the next few minutes walking her through the process. He suggested which paint to purchase, and based on the description of the walls she planned to paint, told her how much paint to buy. While a store employee mixed the color, he steered her toward the aisle of supplies. They added a drop cloth, painter's tape, and brushes to the cart. She paid close attention to his advice and did this cute thing where she wrinkled her brow and placed a manicured nail between her teeth, concentrating hard and interrupting with questions every now and again.

"Remember," he said, wrapping up, "the key is to be organized and take your time. Keep a damp rag handy so if you mess up, you can wipe off the paint while it's wet." Tomas picked up a brush and added it to the cart. "You should get one of these, too. It's an angle brush for the corners and edges."

Talia pursed her lips. "There's more to painting than I thought."

"It's not hard, but you have to know what you're doing. Now you have all the right tools."

She took stock of the items in the cart and then picked up a roller from one of the shelves. "I'm sure there's a technique for using this thing, right?"

"This thing will save you a lot of time." He snatched it from her hand and she playfully wrinkled her nose at him. "This is what you do. First of all, do not dip the roller in the paint or you'll get too much paint on one side and it'll clump on the wall. What you want to do is slowly slide the roller into the paint and use the back of the tray to roll the color along the brush for an even coat. Then, you do this." In the air, he demonstrated how she should roll the color onto the wall.

"Okay, let me try." She took the brush. "Like this?" She did a poor job of mimicking the movements.

"Make a W and then fill it in." He scooted behind her, getting all up on her. Completely unnecessary, but he couldn't seem to help himself. He grasped her wrist, and a charge ricocheted through his blood, shaking him to the core. Her skin was so soft, he thought the contrasting roughness of his hand could bruise her delicate flesh.

Her enticing smell teased his nostrils, a bouquet of rose and jasmine from the fragrance she always wore. But standing so close the floral notes were even stronger, and another scent invaded his senses. He concluded it came from her hair. More subtle, layered under the perfume. Rosemary and…mint? He bent his head for a better whiff when she looked over her shoulder at him.

"I'm ready."

His gut clenched. A perfectly innocent remark, yet powerful arousal lanced through him. She looked up at him through curled lashes, her unconsciously seductive expression wreaking havoc with his libido. If she was ready, he was ready to give it to her.

He swallowed past his parched throat. "Okay...so...use this motion." He didn't recognize the sound of his own voice, it was so raspy.

If she stepped back she'd encounter the hard granite between his legs. He didn't know how he managed to concentrate enough to give her proper instructions, but he struggled through.

"Thank you," she said when they finished. "You're not so bad after all."

"Wish I could say the same." She stuck out her tongue and his shaft jumped. He picked up the filters from a shelf where he'd laid them and held the package in front of his crotch. "Next time, come appropriately dressed. This is a hardware store, not a fashion show."

"These are old clothes." She looked down at the outfit.

He took a good look at her. "I'm not fooled. Those shoes probably cost more than half my wardrobe."

"Can't argue with your comment, since most of your wardrobe consists of T-shirts."

"They're multi-purpose and comfortable," he informed her.

"And cheap."

"That, too." He laughed. "One of these days, I'll let you wear one." Where'd that come from?

Her eyes widened, and awareness crackled between them. She dragged the moist tip of her tongue along the outer edge of her full mouth, prompting an image of him sliding between those full lips. He pushed harder, edged closer. Testing her.

"You're so petite," he said, dropping his voice lower. "I bet if you wore one of my T-shirts it would fit like a short dress."

She swallowed. "Why would I ever wear one of your T-shirts?" she asked in a husky voice.

He shrugged. "Who knows, I may let you borrow one, or you might do something to earn the privilege." His nostrils flared at the thought of her walking around in his clothes. An image of her in his house, in his shirt, with nothing underneath but her warm, sexy body flashed through his brain. He continued to push. "The hem would probably land right here."

He jabbed the air beside her thigh. He didn't touch her, but she jumped back as though electrocuted, and he heard her breath quicken. The sexual tension between them escalated, and they stared each other down. He wanted nothing more than to put her in his car and discover other, more intimate ways to make her breath quicken.

"Excuse me!"

A brusque female voice shattered the tension-filled moment. A harried woman with a baby in a shopping cart and a toddler beside her glared at them. By the pinched expression on her face, Tomas suspected she'd been standing there for a while, ignored in their absorption of each other. They stepped aside so she could pass down the aisle.

Talia fingered the gold loop in her ear. "Thank you for your help." Her overly bright smile signaled the moment had passed and couldn't be recaptured.

"Anytime. I'll even paint if you want. Free of charge." For some reason he couldn't leave well enough. She was about to slip away, and he almost offered to paint her entire house and all the houses in her neighborhood. Because like any red-blooded man about to lose what he desired, all he knew to do was give chase.

"I'll keep that mind. Thanks again."

She eased past him, and he kept her in his sight until she vanished around the corner. He stroked his jaw and walked slowly toward the cash registers at the front of the store.

Talia Jackson was getting under his skin, and he definitely wanted to get to know her better. Now he had to figure out how to make that happen.

Chapter Six

Chin in hand, Talia tried once again to focus on the contracts on her desk. Her Monday morning had started badly. The legal department had sent their recommendations for changes, but she had no better understanding of what the pages in front of her said than she did an hour ago.

Under normal circumstances she focused easily on her job, but today she found it impossible. All morning her mind had wandered. She dreaded seeing Carter in the halls because of the confrontation on Saturday—the drawback of working with someone she used to be married to. With his office a floor below, she hadn't seen him so far, but she didn't know how much longer that would last.

Then the other issue. Tomas. She couldn't get him off her mind. They'd always given each other wide berth, not getting too close. He'd never actually been mean to her, but they had a strange rapport going which included insults, verbal jabs, and then carrying on like it was no big deal. Their relationship had shifted this weekend—at least it seemed that way to her—and she couldn't stop thinking about him. Every time she did, her stomach dropped and left her in a mildly breathless state—not unlike the sensation of a three-hundred-foot plunge on a rollercoaster caused.

Someone rapped at her office door. "Come in."

Lillian, her assistant, walked in with several sheets of paper in her hand and a hesitancy in her step. The brunette had been Talia's assistant for the past few years and moved up to the executive offices when Talia did, too. They worked well together. Lillian understood Talia's temperament and didn't take her occasional snapping and ranting personally. She kept Talia organized and in return, Talia gave her time off whenever she needed it, usually because of one thing or another concerning her children. Parent-teacher conferences and childhood illnesses kept her busy, and as a single mother Lillian didn't have much help. Talia sympathized and did what she could to help her balance work and home.

Talia's gaze followed her assistant until she came to a standstill in front of the desk.

New furniture had been one of the perks of the promotion. As the senior vice president of creative services, she could have chosen any of the more modern designs of glass and chrome like her male counterparts, but she'd settled on a warm cherry wood desk with clean lines and matching cabinets with frosted glass doors.

"A few of us put something together, and we wanted you to take a look," Lillian said.

"What is it?"

Lillian took a deep breath. "You said if I prepared a plan for a company daycare, you'd review it."

Talia had made the off-hand remark in answer to Lillian's request that perhaps she could lobby the owner for an on-site daycare sponsored by the company. She hadn't expected Lillian to actually put together a proposal. One of the negatives of being the only woman on the executive team meant the female staff made requests of her because they assumed she understood their plight.

She held out her hand. "Let me see."

Lillian handed her the sheets of paper stapled together and waited with hands clasped in front of her. The proposal contained neatly typed paragraphs and a budget illustrated with a table and pie chart.

"Where did you get these numbers?" Talia asked.

"We found the averages online."

She glanced up from the sheet. "Jay's not going to accept averages," she said before returning her eyes to the document. She circled the numbers and wrote "be specific" to the side. She flipped to the next page and perused the contents. Overall, the proposal was a decent plan to get the point across but needed more detail. She wrote notes and suggestions in the margin and crossed out a few sentences before handing the pages back to Lillian.

"Add in the info I requested and delete the mushy stuff I crossed out. Jay is logical and he only cares about how much this is going to cost and whether or not the cost is worth the investment." Lillian nodded her understanding and Talia decided to go all in. What the hell. "Make the changes and I'll take the proposal to him and see if I can convince him to set up the daycare."

Lillian squealed. "Yes! Thank you, Talia."

"I'm *presenting* it, Lillian. There are no guarantees."

"I know, I know, but thanks. It's great having a woman on the team, you know? Someone who looks out for our interests. And I know you don't have kids or anything and you're a busy executive, but you understand how difficult it is for those of us who do have children. Thank you so much."

Her enthusiastic response made Talia feel guilty she hadn't taken the project seriously in the first place. She saw how the single mothers struggled, and even the married ones tended to be the primary caregivers and had a hard time balancing work and their kids. How many of them had been overlooked for promotions and special projects because of assumptions they didn't have the same work ethic as the men or couldn't accommodate the late night work schedules and the trips out of town?

Lillian danced toward the door, and speak of the devil, Jay came in as she was leaving.

"Hi, Mr. Santorini," Lillian sang, grinning

from ear to ear as she closed the door behind her.

"What's going on with her?"

"She's excited about a project she's working on." Talia stood. "Aren't you supposed to be in Italy?"

Jay Santorini wore a white pullover shirt and dark pants. Not part of the typical office dress code, so she knew he'd only dropped in for a short visit. His father had started the company and turned over control to Jay when he retired. Despite rumors of being a playboy and a slacker, the company flourished under Jay's leadership.

"Change of plans," he answered. Every year he took whichever woman he considered his latest girlfriend on vacation to his family's villa on Lake Maggiore in Turin, Italy, for two weeks including Memorial Day weekend. "But don't worry, I won't be in your hair all week, either." He waved his hand, indicating she should reclaim her seat and after she did, he settled into the guest chair across from her. "What's the latest with JBC?"

The acronym JBC stood for Johnson Brewing Company out of Seattle, Omega's most recent and well-known client. Omega held the position of largest ad agency in the Southeast, but under normal circumstances they couldn't compete against the national advertising firms out of New York and Los Angeles. Winning JBC's business was a major accomplishment.

Johnson Brewing Company was African-American-owned and one of the largest breweries in the country. For years they'd worked with the same ad agency, but after a loss in market share three years in a row, the family had decided to try other companies and implement a new marketing strategy.

Omega beat out five other firms to win the contract to work with them. Talia supervised the entire creative department and her responsibilities included making sure all the ad campaigns fit within client guidelines. She knew Jay trusted her, but because of the massive rebranding of JBC, he paid closer attention to the goings on than he normally did.

"We're making headway," Talia said. "Cyrus, the oldest Johnson son and the head of the company, is due in town on business in a couple of weeks and wants to come by the office to meet the team."

"Does he like what we've presented so far?" Jay asked.

"So far so good."

"All right. Keep me informed." He rose from the chair and walked back to the door but stopped halfway there. "Everything okay with you?" he asked.

She glanced up in surprise. Generally speaking, Jay didn't get personal, but she had no doubt his question referred to Carter bringing Paula to the company picnic, a topic she didn't want to discuss with her boss. "I'm fine."

"You don't need time off? Because if you do, I'd understand."

"We're in the middle of an important campaign, Jay. Why would I take time off?" She didn't take time off. Even more so now because she couldn't afford the luxury of sitting idle with her own thoughts. Then she'd have to admit how empty her life was.

He shrugged, looking at the far wall. "I guess you're stronger than me. When my wife and I divorced nine years ago, I took a week off. I didn't come to work and didn't want to see anyone. Lucky for me, we didn't work together." His gaze met hers again. "Something to think about."

Talia kept her features neutral. "Thank you."

He opened his mouth, apparently to add an additional comment, but changed his mind and walked out.

When the door shut, Talia's shoulders drooped and she buried her face in her hands. With everyone treating her like a fragile piece of glass, she was starting to feel fragile. Work provided a refuge. It always had. And since she and Carter split, it had become even more important.

The clock on her desk read almost lunch time. Maybe getting out for a bit would do her some good. She grabbed her purse and took the elevator to street level, but on the way down she changed her mind about eating in the building's café.

She went through the revolving door and right away experienced a burst of energy like she always did when she walked around downtown Atlanta. Workers traipsed along the busy sidewalk on their way to lunch with co-workers or ran errands during the short window of time before they had to return to work. Tourists snapped photos or fumbled with maps as they took in the sights.

She kept walking, not sure where she was headed until she came to an intersection and realized she was on her way to a restaurant she hadn't been to in a long time. As she waited for the light to change with a half dozen or so other people, she heard a voice behind her.

"I couldn't be so lucky again."

Warm ripples raced down her spine.

Tomas stood behind her. Seeing his smiling face buoyed her spirits, but she didn't bother to analyze the meaning of such a shift in attitude and fought the goofy grin that threatened to spread across her face.

The sun glinted off the natural blonde highlights in his hair, and he ran his fingers through it, sending the silky strands rippling through his fingers as he pushed them back from his forehead, giving her a good look at his handsome face. A truly beautiful man—classically handsome with high cheekbones, a square jaw, and a prominent nose just the right size for his face. He seemed oblivious to the looks that came his way as they stood there, but she saw them. She couldn't blame the women for staring and doing double takes. He exemplified the type of rugged perfection most women fantasized about, and she found it harder and harder to control this newfound attraction that burdened her each time they met.

She'd been so caught up in his appearance she hadn't noticed he wasn't alone. Two men stood alongside him wearing similar clothing—jeans, T-shirts, and dusty work boots.

Finally getting her bearings, Talia found the

wherewithal to talk. "What are you doing in my neck of the woods?" she asked. "Shouldn't you be off somewhere pounding nails and cutting wood?"

"We had business at the zoning office and thought we'd grab a bite to eat while down here," Tomas replied. "Any suggestions?"

The light changed and people started moving, steering around them since they blocked the crosswalk.

"There's plenty, but it depends on what you want. If you'd like sandwiches, there's a great place in the building over there." She pointed across the street. "Their Reuben sandwiches are to die for. They're stuffed full of meat and a special sauce created by the owner. There's also a pretty good Brazilian place a couple of blocks up on the right."

"Are you headed to lunch?"

"Yes."

He spoke in Spanish to the men with him. They ogled her and used the word *morena*, which she knew could mean dark-skinned. That let her know they were discussing her, but she didn't comprehend much else. Her high school Spanish was no match for their fast talking and advanced vocabulary.

After the men walked away, Tomas turned to her. "Let's go," he said.

"Excuse me?" Talia put a hand on her hip and cocked her head as if she didn't hear him.

"I'm going to lunch with you."

"I didn't invite you."

"I know. I'm inviting you."

"Well, shouldn't you wait for me to say yes?"

He started across the street, and after hesitating in stunned silence, Talia hurried after him.

"Where are we going?" he asked.

She gave up and went along with his steamroller behavior. Besides, she didn't mind the company. "To get Indian food."

He wrinkled his nose, which was kind of adorable on a man with his masculine features. "Never had it."

"There's a first time for everything, and that's what I'm in the mood for."

He grunted.

"Don't be such a baby," she said.

"It better be good."

"It will be." They approached the door of the restaurant and she turned around to smile at him. "I promise."

She didn't know why she did that. Maybe because he'd told her to smile more, and being in his presence made her *want* to smile more. He reached above her head and pulled the door wider, getting much closer than he needed to. He looked down at her with a sexy half grin that made her heart jump and private parts of her anatomy tighten in unexpected awareness.

"Promises, promises," he said.

Chapter Seven

He was going to fuck her. He didn't know when and didn't know how, but it would definitely happen. If Talia kept smiling at him like that it would happen sooner rather than later.

Her hair fell past her shoulder blades in a luxurious mass, looking like she'd stepped out of a salon moments before. What he wouldn't give to clench a handful of those locks and tug her head back to the perfect angle so he could taste the smooth lines of her throat. Her tempting bottom and curvaceous hips moved back and forth in front of him in a tangerine-colored sheath dress. The movement, not in the least bit overtly sexual, managed to be so nonetheless.

He loved women, but he drew the line at sleeping with another man's wife and had never had an affair with a married woman—not knowingly, anyway. So he hadn't considered her fair game. Now she was free, all bets were off.

When they did the deed, he would have her wear the same black heels she had on today with the straps crisscrossed over her ankles. Imagining her in his bed, legs in the air, wearing those sexy shoes made his groin muscles constrict so tightly it became difficult to walk without discomfort.

An Indian woman dressed in a blue and gold sari led the way through the tables filled with diners. Cinnamon, cumin, curry—and other spices not so familiar—permeated the air. She seated them near the back in a booth with red seats and handed them menus.

Tomas set his aside. "What do you suggest?" he asked.

"Are you okay with spicy food?"

He leaned back and spread one arm along the back of the booth. He had to concentrate not to stare at her mouth.

"Of course. I'm Cuban."

"Not all Hispanic people like spicy food, and I didn't want to assume." She perused the menu.

"You're trying to be politically correct with me? Thank you, I appreciate it, but it's not necessary. I've heard all kinds of things, believe me."

She looked up. "Like what?"

"Like people assuming I came here by boat and got to stay under the wet foot dry foot policy."

She frowned. "Um, didn't you? I thought—"

"Yes, I did, but that doesn't mean they have to assume it."

She giggled. There that smile again, lighting up her eyes and face. Yeah, he was going to fuck her.

"The trip must have been scary," she said.

He nodded. "There were fourteen of us on a small boat, mostly men, but a couple of women and a little girl only ten years old. When we landed, we were almost out of food. We only had a few pieces of stale bread left, some fruit, and less than a liter of water. A few times I doubted we'd survive the trip, but we did. *Gracias a Dios.*" He kissed the gold cross on his neck. "What had kept me, kept all of us going, was the hope of finding a better life in the United States. Worth the risk, even though we could be turned back or even worse, die at sea."

He'd made up his mind that if they didn't manage to slip by the U.S. Coast Guard, he would try to enter through Mexico, another route some Cubans took to enter the country. As long as he had breath in his body, he had intended to make it onto American soil. Not only for himself, but for his family back home.

"So all your family is still in Cuba?"

"Most. I have an aunt in New York, and cousins scattered in Florida and on other Caribbean islands. I'm not close to them, though. My mother and my two younger brothers live in Santa Clara, where I'm from. I had an older brother…" His throat constricted. He didn't talk about his brother much, but he'd idolized him, and every time he mentioned Manuel, he experienced a wave of grief that never failed to take him unawares.

Talia's small hand covered his on the table and squeezed before she withdrew. The brief contact comforted him, and he pressed on, the empathy in her eyes filling him with an urge to tell the rest of the story.

"My brother, Manuel, tried to come here before me. The smartest one in our family, he always made good grades in school and enjoyed science and math. We knew he would do big things if he could make it to this country and take advantage of the opportunities the United States offered, but he didn't make it." Ten years had passed and still his brother's death remained an ache in his gut, almost as fresh as the day he learned of his passing. His mother had collapsed and didn't leave her bed for days when they received the devastating news.

He shifted in the chair and rubbed his hands on his thighs to regain his composure. "As the second oldest, I offered to come next. My mother begged me not to after what happened, but I wanted to finish what he didn't. She's raising Manuel's two kids now."

Talia's eyes filled with sadness. "I'm sorry about your brother."

"It happened a long time ago," Tomas said.

"But we never recover from the death of a loved one, do we? No matter the circumstances or when it happened."

Her voice softened and sounded pained. He suspected she was very familiar with the loss of someone she cared deeply about.

The waiter arrived and he let her order for him. She requested samosas filled with meat to start, insisting he try them because of their similarity to *empanadas*. She ordered him a plate of lamb vindaloo, described as a spicy dish with potatoes and a splash of lemon juice. For her, chicken tikka nestled in a rich tomato cream sauce.

The food arrived piping hot in stainless steel serving dishes. The enticing aroma whet his appetite and he dug in, heaping spoonfuls of basmati rice and vegetables onto his plate. Each bite seemed better than the last, and he wolfed down the meal. He ate most of the naan bread himself, and not wanting to leave a single morsel behind, used the last piece to sop up every bit of the spicy curry sauce on his plate.

At the end of the meal, he patted his stomach. "Delicious."

"I told you."

"So you were right once in your life. There's a first time for everything."

She pursed her lips. "You refuse to give me one little bit of credit."

Tomas threw up his hands. "All right, fine. You were right. I can't believe I never tried Indian food before. Happy now?"

"You're welcome," Talia said, her smile triumphant.

Tomas drained the last of the mango lassi from his glass. "So, are you coming to my picnic on Saturday?"

"You really do want me to come," she said, sounding smug. "I should let you suffer without my presence." She rested her chin on her hand.

"Don't get a big head, Talia. I just think you need it."

"Oh really?" She tilted her head. "Something else I need, according to you. You're quite the expert on me and my needs."

He planned to be. "The fresh air will do you good."

"I prefer my air filled with all the smoggy goodness of car fumes, thank you very much. I can't think of any reason why I'd want to drive that far outside of the city with all the mosquitoes and bugs. Ugh." She shivered.

He folded his arms on the table, watching her twirl a strand of hair around her index finger. "Aren't you from Georgia?"

"Yes, but I've lived in Atlanta—the city—all my life. There's a difference."

She had attractive features and was quite pretty, with long lashes curled at the ends and smoky, dark brown eyes. He didn't say anything else for awhile, wondering what it would take to get her alone and how receptive she'd be to the opportunity. He watched her until she fidgeted and played with the earring in her ear, gaze bouncing from him to the table and back again.

"So you really renovated the house all by yourself?" she asked.

She was referring to the property he'd purchased out in the country and now lived in. "Pretty much. You should come see it."

He kept his voice even, firm, as if to imply she had no other choice but to obey. He didn't often take women to his house because they couldn't appreciate the tranquility of the country. His closest neighbor lived miles away, and he was glad for the distance between them. Before he left Cuba, citizens didn't have the right to own and sell property. The laws were changing, but it was nothing like here. He was proud of his place and the fact he could call it his own.

"I'll think about coming out this weekend," Talia said.

She broke the link of their connected gazes by picking up the ticket the waiter had placed there minutes before.

"What are you doing?" Tomas demanded.

"I'm getting the check."

He snatched it away and leaned across the table. "What kind of *pendejo* would I be to let you pay, especially after I invited you to lunch?"

Her mouth fell open. "I assumed—"

"That's the problem. Too much assuming." He winked to let her know he was joking and slid from the booth. "Come on. I can't spend all day here with you. I have to get back to work."

Talia followed him to the front where he paid the bill with cash, and she waited at the door when he went back to the table to leave a tip.

"Thank you for lunch," she said once they were walking back the way they came.

"You're welcome."

They fell silent. She'd been enjoying herself and hadn't thought about work or the mess of her life during the entire hour. She wanted to walk slowly to prolong their time together, but his long-legged strides made it impossible to do.

"Is this part of the truce?" she asked lightly, reminding him of his request at the housewarming party.

He chuckled. "It could be. You're not as bad as I thought."

"Me?" she huffed. "Huh."

They came to the intersection where she had

to veer right to get back to her building. "I'm going this way. I work on the top floor over there." She pointed to the gray stone building. "You're headed back to the work site?"

He nodded but seemed hesitant to leave. Parting ways was turning into an inelegant process, and the thought that he wanted to delay saying goodbye as much as she did was at once peculiarly electrifying and disquieting.

"I'll see you around," Talia said.

"Maybe this weekend? There'll be plenty of food."

"But no drama?" She immediately regretted the comment and the negative memories it conjured. "I shouldn't have said that."

"What you said doesn't bother me. You think too much." He took a look at his watch. "I better go."

"Bye."

"Hey." He caught her wrist, halting her retreat. Goose flesh pimpled the length of her arm. Her body's reaction startled her.

She squinted against the sun peering over his broad shoulders. They were standing at an incline on the sidewalk, so he loomed even taller than usual above her. His eyes were framed by long, sooty lashes, and they were almost as clear as glass, pulling her into their depths.

His lips weren't particularly full, but their sensual lines promised passion and pleasure and from what she'd heard, it would not be false advertising. She could only imagine the ways in which those lips could make a woman lose her inhibitions and beg for more.

"I had a good time with you today," he said. "Thanks for introducing me to Indian food. Enjoy your afternoon."

Before he released her, he rubbed his thumb along the inside of her wrist. She imagined the same calloused skin rasping across her nipples, and her pulse went berserk.

He released her as suddenly as he'd grabbed her, and then he walked away, crossing the street to the other side. His broad back disappeared between the ebb and flow of pedestrian traffic. Meanwhile, she couldn't move. Her heart beat quickly from the alarming thought that had raced through her mind when he held onto her. She turned in the direction of her office building, confused by the turn of events.

She'd wanted more than his hand on her wrist. She'd wanted him to kiss her.

Chapter Eight

Memorial Day weekend. Backyard barbeque. Salsa music blasting from wireless speakers. Nothing like good food, music, and friends to remind a person of the important things in life.

Tomas carted a tub filled with ice, sodas, and beer out to the back yard and set it against the side of the house. Dozens of people occupied the wooded property. Some sat around tables playing dominoes and cards. Children chased each other and played hide-and-seek, using the scarlet oak and dogwood trees dotting the yard as hiding places.

He'd bought this place on a whim. At the time, the house had been in a shabby state and the grounds overrun with weeds. From what he understood, no one had made an offer on it in over a year. By the time he and the real estate agent completed the as-is sale, he'd purchased the property at fifty-percent below market value. The bank had practically thrown it at him.

A few friends thought he was a sucker for buying it, but with the house fixed up, no one could deny its beauty. Working off and on while commuting from his apartment, it had taken a long time to get the property to its current state. He'd gutted the entire inside and renovated the sprawling ranch into a four-bedroom with an eat-in kitchen. Even better, he could proudly say he'd done most of the work himself.

Coming home after a long day of work was like finding peace in a storm, and problems lost their importance once he drove up the dirt road to the front door. He would sit on the porch with his feet propped up, sipping a beer or an iced tea—depending on his mood—and stare out at the still waters of his very own lake.

He couldn't believe how far he'd come since Santa Clara, Cuba.

"Oh good, more drinks!" someone squealed. Three scantily clad women bum-rushed him and each grabbed a can from the tub. They wore almost identical cut off shorts and tube tops. He wasn't sure who they were or who they'd arrived with, but they were a welcome addition to the festivities.

"*Gracias*, Tomas," one of them said, batting her lashes at him.

"You can thank me properly later," he quipped. She giggled and walked away. He'd had his eye on her friend, but if she wanted to show her gratitude, he wasn't opposed to it.

He rejoined his buddy Ryan at one of the

outside tables and sat where he'd left his plate of food. Ryan was eating a hamburger and keeping an eye on a group of kids on the tire swing near the lake.

"When does Shawna get here?" Tomas asked. Ryan had come over early to help him set up and get started on the grilling so there'd be food ready when the first guests arrived.

"In a few. She should be here any minute now."

Tomas pointed. "There she is."

He paused, pleasantly surprised when he saw Talia followed behind Shawna, who had her hands full with Madison and the diaper bag slung over her shoulder. Ryker ran ahead of them to join other kids playing with a puppy someone had brought. What had prompted Talia to show up? Although he'd pushed for her to come, he never had the impression she actually would.

A pair of designer sunglasses with detailing on the temples perched on her head, and her colorful, strapless dress left her shoulders bare for his hungry gaze. Today she seemed sullen, as if some problem or issue weighed on her mind. When she glanced in his direction, he held her gaze for several moments before she looked away.

"Don't mess with her," Ryan warned, having seen the look they exchanged.

Am I really that bad? Tomas wondered. "Something's wrong," he said.

Shawna and Talia came over and greeted them, and both men stood to give them their chairs.

"Keep your seats," Shawna said with a wave of her hand. "I'm going into the kitchen to warm Madison's bottle."

Tomas's gaze fell on Talia. "What are you doing here? Are you lost?"

Shawna answered before she could. "Leave her alone. She's had a rough day."

"Oh really? Then I should be flattered and honored you dragged yourself all the way out here to my little home," he said.

"You should be flattered and honored every time I'm in your presence," Talia said.

Tomas chuckled and tilted the chair back on two legs, affecting a relaxed pose but acutely aware of her. His gaze strolled from her kissable-looking shoulders to her delicate ankles. Being a devoted fan of all things female, he noticed how the strapless dress skimmed her curves and showed off the tempting rise of her breasts. Again she wore heels, making her shapely legs look longer and laying bare manicured toes painted an electric blue. An unusual but interesting choice.

"Oh, I am flattered and honored," he said with a lazy drawl. "*Mi casa es su casa.* Help yourself to anything you want." He waved his hand with a flourish.

"That's awfully generous of you. Anything?"

His steady gaze locked on her. "Anything."

Heat flickered in her eyes before they skirted to the table. The teasing between them had escalated to full-on flirting, but she must not be completely comfortable in the new role. Probably because it had been a while since she'd had to pull a man in. Certainly not while she was married, but with her body she had the tools to do it.

Recently divorced women were a unique breed. Seldom in a rush to get into another serious relationship, they presented the perfect opportunity for a short fling.

"I'll keep that in mind. For when I want something," Talia said, facing him boldly now.

Their friends watched the exchange between them closely, and from their raised brows, he suspected they were just as intrigued by the conversation as he.

He let his gaze lower to her mouth. She wore a shade of lipstick slightly lighter than her skin, drawing attention to the bee-stung temptation of her full lips. He pushed his hair back from his face and her gaze lifted to follow the movement. His throat seized and his hand paused for a fraction of a second before falling away. He knew women, and there was no mistaking the look she sent him. He recognized lust when he saw it.

"When you want something, don't be shy. Make sure you ask for it." He saw the heat in her eyes again, but this time she didn't look away.

"I'm going inside to warm the bottle," Shawna announced, grabbing Talia's wrist and dragging her toward the house.

Ryan leaned toward Tomas. "Okay, I know you pretended to be her man at the housewarming party, but tell me the truth. Is there something going on between you two?"

Tomas turned to his friend. "Not yet."

Chapter Nine

Talia observed Tomas out the kitchen window. Funny how you could see someone and not pay much attention to them. Then one day, the blinders come off and all the characteristics you'd overlooked suddenly become apparent. He used to annoy the hell out of her, though she'd be a liar if she claimed not to have noticed his physical appeal. Overall, she saw him with new eyes now.

She'd never had any desire to venture this far out into the "boonies" before, where the houses were few and far between, but all of a sudden she was glad she'd called Shawna and invited herself on the hour-long drive. She took a swallow from the can of soda she picked up on the way inside.

"Stop looking at him," Shawna said from behind her.

"Nothing wrong with looking," Talia responded. She turned away from the window.

To get to the kitchen, she and Shawna had passed the living room and she'd hung back to take a peek, curious to get a better handle on Tomas and his personality. The room was filled with large, traditional furniture in dark hues. A chocolate couch and a black leather recliner with a cup holder had clearly seen better days but looked comfy. He had a collection of miniature classic cars stacked on shelves behind a locked glass case that loomed almost to the ceiling. The floors looked like the original hardwood had been stripped and refinished so they gleamed under the overhead lights, and in front of the fireplace a beige area rug with running horses on it added a warm accent to the masculine room.

Above the fireplace mantle, an enlarged photo hung in a gold frame. A considerably younger looking Tomas, perhaps in his late teens and with longer hair, smiled with people she assumed must be his mother and three brothers. The boys all looked alike, each good-looking in his own way, though Tomas stood out because of his lighter colored eyes. His parents had blessed the world with four handsome young men.

When she'd entered the enormous eat-in kitchen, Talia had placed her purse on the table and walked over to run her hand along the six-burner Viking range, which suggested Tomas had a love of cooking. Surprising, as she'd never expected him to be the cooking type. Where she'd gone for light and bright in her own kitchen, he'd chosen walnut cabinets and polished steel handles. Being nosy, she'd opened the Viking refrigerator and found it filled with foodstuffs—fruits, vegetables, juices and the like. Clearly Tomas would never starve to death out here far from civilization.

With Madison on her hip, Shawna stood at the counter fiddling with the bottle warmer. Madison babbled happily, as if she knew she was about to be fed. "You know what kind of guy he is. He's a flirt and a womanizer," Shawna said.

"I don't want to sleep with him." Not entirely true. The more she thought about it, the more attractive the idea became.

"I hope not. What you're going through will pass. Divorce is not the end of the world."

"I hate the word divorce," Talia said. Her throat tightened. "Such an ugly word. I still haven't gotten used to the idea that I'm actually a divorcée. I never thought I'd be in this situation after being married so long." Even in the last days, when her marriage ran on fumes and she and Carter slept in separate bedrooms, she hadn't expected this end result. "The ink barely dried on our divorce papers before Carter started seeing that woman. She's twenty-one years his junior. Barely out of diapers! And you know what he said to me today?" Her neck muscles tensed as she thought about his visit to her condo. He'd come by to drop off a box of her personal items accidentally left at the house when she'd moved out.

"No, what?" Shawna somehow managed to lift the bottle from the warmer and test the warmth of the contents on her opposite wrist, all while balancing her wriggling daughter in her arms. Mothers were a rare breed of magician.

"He said, 'There's something I need to tell you and I wanted you to hear it from me first. Paula and I are getting married.' I swear I almost hit him, but I gave him a good piece of my mind. I tossed out every curse word I could think of and told him to never speak to me again." The speed with which she'd been replaced still lingered like the aftertaste of a bitter pill.

"Since you work together, that won't be easy," Shawna said reasonably.

Talia huffed. "I don't have anything to say to him, and I don't want him to say anything to me." She pretended to study her manicure. "Do you think he was seeing her before we divorced?" she asked quietly.

"I don't know, Talia. He said he wasn't."

They hadn't made love in over a year before the divorce, no longer able to summon the energy or strength to feign interest in a physical relationship when the emotional one had deteriorated so spectacularly. She had been celibate, but there was no guarantee he'd been.

"Whether he did or didn't doesn't matter now anyway," she announced. "I'm divorced, not dead, and it's time I get my groove back."

"Please tell me you're not thinking of getting it back with Tomas."

"Why not? He's single, I'm single. Tomas fits the bill, and you're right, I already know what kind of man he is." She'd seen his flirtations, and Shawna had told her about his escapades with numerous women over the years. "I'm not looking for another husband."

"Your ex-husband has moved on, and so will

you—when the time is right." Shawna could always be counted on to be reasonable and careful.

"What if the time to move on is right now?" Talia asked.

Shawna sat down in one of the chairs around the table, her daughter in one hand and the bottle in the other. Madison took the bottle and gulped greedily. "You just got divorced."

"So did Carter." Talia crossed her arms over her chest.

"But you're not him. Give yourself time. What's the rush?"

"You're the most cautious person I know. I probably shouldn't take advice from you." Talia softened the comment with a grin.

Unable to deny the truth, Shawna smiled wryly. "Fair enough, but how about this? If you want to start dating right away, let me introduce you to a few of Ryan's other friends. Or try dating online. Cara found the man she's seeing on one of those singles sites. It took a few tries, but they seem to be a perfect match."

Talia returned her attention to the scene outside the window. "Hmm...I don't know."

The thought of setting up an online dating profile and fielding offers from amorous men who may or may not be truthful about the details they shared didn't appeal to her. It meant entering the unknown, and she wasn't so sure she had the desire to go through the trouble.

"Anybody but Tomas. He's dangerous and you're vulnerable," Shawna warned.

"Dangerous?" Talia laughed. "Don't worry. I

can handle myself. Besides, how bad could he be?"

"Real bad. Don't get me wrong, I love Tomas, but I don't know what it is, he gets women to do all kinds of crazy things. They simply forget who they are. He says he moved out to the country because he likes the slower pace, but sometimes I wonder if it's because he wants to avoid the hordes of women who hound him. He has restraining orders against at least two of them."

"Now you've got me even more curious," Talia murmured.

"What?" Shawna asked sharply.

"You heard me."

"I see the way you're looking at him. Stay away from him. He's absolutely the wrong man for you."

Talia studied Tomas, sitting with his legs spread wide, arms crossed over his chest. He didn't have to move—or do anything, in fact, to have women gravitate to him. Since she'd returned her attention to the window, two had approached, flirtatiously touching his arm. One had gone so far as to play in the hair brushing his shoulder.

A mild pulse of awareness filled her. She twirled a lock of hair around her finger. She wanted to be like those women—to touch him, his hair, and his hard body. And she wanted him to touch her, to explore and make her feel alive and desirable again. She hadn't had her sexual needs tended to in so long, and he would know what to do.

Tomas might be the wrong man for a long-term relationship, but he was the right man for what she had in mind.

****

Hours later, when darkness fell and guests started to leave, Talia lingered. Luckily she'd followed Shawna in her own vehicle, so when her friend was ready to go, she made up an excuse to stay behind. Shawna sent her a warning look, but she didn't say much else before she and Ryan left.

Talia helped with the clean up, clearing dishes, tied up trash bags, and did whatever she could to delay her departure. When the last of the stragglers had gone, she went into the kitchen and wiped down the counters. Covered leftovers were put away in the refrigerator and then she focused on washing pots, pans, and utensils while Tomas finished up outside.

She had put away the last of the dishes and was wiping her hands on a towel when she sensed him behind her. She turned to see him leaning against the doorjamb with a Corona in his hand, watching. He did that a lot. Observing, paying attention to people as if turning things over in his mind. As she was the only one there, she was the focus of his watchful gaze. How long he'd been standing in the doorway, she had no idea.

Seconds dragged by and neither of them made a sound.

He walked slowly toward her, and the closer he came, the louder her heart beat. Now she was about to execute her plan of seduction, she became extremely nervous. Her mouth dried and butterflies filled her stomach. An irrational need to bolt surged through her, but she suppressed it.

She hadn't stayed behind only to succumb to nerves.

"All done in here," she said in her brightest voice, but it sounded false and nervous.

"Thank you for your help. You didn't have to wash the dishes."

She shrugged. "I wanted to."

He tipped the beer toward her, but she declined his offer with a shake of her head. He upturned the bottle and chugged the remnants, the entire time keeping his eyes on her. His Adam's apple bobbed once, twice as he swallowed. Even when he set the empty bottle on the counter he didn't take his eyes from her.

He tilted his head to the side. "Why are you still here, Talia?"

She swallowed and had the distinct feeling that because she was out of practice, she was unprepared for what was to come. She seldom felt out of her depth, but he was so big, so virile, so unapologetically male. "I wanted to help you."

He studied her with an intense, probing look. "Just being helpful?"

"Yes," she whispered.

"I didn't think you knew how to do household chores."

"I didn't have to growing up. We always had hired help..." He raised his brows, and she realized how pretentious she sounded. "I do know how to clean up," she insisted, a defensive note to her voice. "I just don't have to because—"

"Because you have someone else to do it."

His gaze skipped to the front of her dress, doing that thing he did, undressing her with his eyes so she felt naked. He was so brazen about it; it was obvious he didn't give a damn if she noticed. Her breasts suddenly became heavy, as if weighted down with a foreign substance.

He came closer, invading her personal space. The temperature in the room rose to scorching as his focus moved to her mouth. "You have nice lips."

She felt like a gazelle being stalked by a lion, waiting, wondering when it would pounce. Lust coiled in her loins as high voltage electricity surrounded them, and her nipples throbbed and jutted against her dress. It had been a long time since she'd felt sexual in any kind of way. She laughed to ease the tension, her heart fluttering like the violent flap of a bird's wings.

"You should see pictures of me as a child. I had to grow into these lips." She touched her fingers to her mouth.

The corners of his lips didn't budge, not even a fraction. "I'm going to kiss you," he said calmly. "Do you have a problem with that?"

She couldn't move, could hardly breathe. Helplessly frozen as if bound by ropes. What breaths she did take were filled with the scent of him. "No."

It's what she'd been hoping for, what she'd wanted, why she'd stayed behind under the pretense of being helpful. She wanted kisses and much, much more.

"I didn't think you would."

His cocky self-confidence should annoy her, but instead it made her hornier. His index finger slowly traced the curve of her jaw line and the outer edge of her bottom lip. The benign touch sizzled across her skin and spurred her heart into a gallop at breakneck speed.

With a hand to her waist, he drew her close, molding her soft curves to the steely strength of his body. He lowered his head and did exactly as he said he would.

From the minute their mouths meshed together she free-falled into the seductive pull of his lips. One large hand cupped her face as if she were made of the finest porcelain, his coarse thumb skimming the surface of her skin beneath the cheekbone. He was gentle at first, but then she edged closer, wanting more than this tender passion as fire licked through her veins with frightening speed.

He let out a low growl, his velvet tongue pushing past her lips to let the crisp bitterness of beer fill her mouth. He kissed with such fervor her head tilted back at a sharp angle. Guiding her to the counter, he tightened his hold. The edge pressed into her back, but no discomfort could distract her from this indelicate raid on her senses.

Tomas angled his head and shifted his hand into her hair. His fingers weaved through the strands to massage her scalp in a circular pattern that sent erotic sensations down to her nape. He traced the corners of her mouth with his tongue, tasting and teasing until she could barely stand the torture, shaking from the force of desire and whimpering in need. His mouth caressed hers, and she felt like she was floating on air, drifting weightlessly upward. She'd never been kissed like this, and she didn't want it to end. Clutching his shoulders, she determined to hold onto him and not let him go if he tried to stop.

He cupped her bottom and massaged the soft flesh, guiding her leg upward so he was in the cradle of her thighs with his hard length pressed into her belly. Passion she hadn't experienced in a long time erupted in her blood, making her feel alive, wide awake and aware of his every touch.

He lowered his lips to her neck, leaving a trail of flames wherever his mouth touched. She gasped when he sucked the engorged nipple of her breast through her bodice. Locking her arms around his neck, she held him in place. Mentally reeling, she moaned at the heightened ache he'd created with such a simple touch. But this was just what she needed. To be wanted with such keen desire nothing else mattered but satisfying it.

Boldly, she lifted his shirt, fingers hunting for the hot, hard flesh of his back. She traced the muscles there and a tremor fizzed through him. When he lifted his head, his need was laid out as plain as writing in his angular face. His clear brown eyes had darkened to chestnut, and his chest expanded with each labored breath.

He didn't say a word. He didn't have to. He simply lifted her in his arms and walked out of the kitchen.

Chapter Ten

As soon as he placed Talia on the carpeted floor of his bedroom, Tomas began to undress. The first item he removed was the T-shirt. Enraptured by the strip tease, Talia watched as each inch of his perfect body was revealed. When he finally shed all his clothes, she stood in admiration of his physique. Confident in his own skin, he waited with aplomb while she scrutinized him from head to toe, a man clearly used to being naked.

Her inspection started at his thick neck and brushed with longing over his golden skin. His muscles had muscles, a body so tight there wasn't an ounce of surplus flesh anywhere. Washboard abs you could literally wash clothes on, broad shoulders and muscled thighs. He resembled a gladiator from centuries gone by, and she easily imagined him in a coliseum fight to the death where he would come out the victor.

Her gaze lowered to his steely length, nestled in a thatch of dark hair and standing straight up. Big. Tremendous.

She swallowed, and when he reached for her, she stepped out of reach. "It's been a while," she said.

"Then we should get you ready." His fingers curled into the fabric of her dress and he pulled her toward him.

As he reached for the zipper at the back, she stayed his hand, suddenly mindful no other man but her ex-husband had seen her naked in over ten years. "The light."

Tomas shook his head. "I want to see all of you. Everything." He lowered his head and kissed her again, softly, soothingly, easing her fears. When he sensed her calm, he lowered the zipper and pulled the dress over her head, tossing it over his shoulder. Next, her underwear and strapless bra.

His appreciative gaze swept over her naked body and she fought the instinctive urge to fold her arms over her front and hide from him. "Beautiful," Tomas murmured. And how could she not feel beautiful, when he looked at her with such desire-filled eyes?

He grazed the tips of her breasts with the back of his hand and the tiny buds tightened painfully.

"Tomas..." she breathed.

Slowly, he urged her backward without touching, his steps deliberate and eyes focused. Her legs bumped the edge of the bed. "What do you want, *querida*?" he whispered, bending close. He'd never called her that before—beloved, darling. She responded to the affection in the words, longing to touch and be touched. "This?"

Lifting her onto the mattress, he fastened his mouth over her breast. She tossed her head back, gasping at the immediate shock of pleasure. He sucked the hard peak and she strained toward him with quivering eagerness. He licked the nipple, laving the tip with moisture, and the sight of his pink tongue flicking over the dark peak made her throb with heated desire. She let him suck and pull, unwilling to do anything but give him the unrestricted right to drive her mad. Inhaling a trembling breath, she filled her fists with strands of his hair, holding on to the brown locks as he gorged in a leisurely fashion, using his tongue and lips to tug and tease.

Then he was cupping her mound, circling her clit, his fingers becoming drenched in moisture as he fondled the plump folds. "Nice and wet, just the way I like," he whispered, spreading warm air over her breast. He lifted his head and locked his eyes with hers. "I want you to touch yourself."

The shocking request left her speechless, and Talia shook her head, curling her hands into themselves—embarrassed and mildly mortified by the request, even as her body creamed in response.

"Relax." Tomas gently released the fingers one by one and guided her hand to the triangle of hair between her legs. "Go ahead. Don't be shy," he coaxed. "I want to watch."

He eased her knees apart and laid her bare, exposed to him. Talia held his steady gaze and hesitantly, haltingly, slid her fingers over the tight pearl between her legs. She was so sensitive there she gasped, and right away became filled with a profound sense of power as she watched his jaw tighten in concentrated focus. His intensity aroused her further and her confidence increased.

Trailing trembling fingers over the wet curls, she stroked tentatively at first and then moved with bolder strokes. As she touched herself, her whole body became awash in sensations. A pounding ache filled her loins and her moans grew louder. She was losing herself, panting heavily as her mind spun in a twisted circle. Her fingers skirted the firm nub couched between the feminine petals, and she became lost in self-stimulation and arched her hips up, sucking in a lungful of air.

Murmuring approval, Tomas dragged her to the edge of the bed by the ankles. Spreading her legs wider, he levered over her and kissed a path along the delicate curve of her stomach. His hand joined hers between her legs, and a soft cry left Talia's throat, her voice pained and unrecognizable.

Tomas dropped to his knees and took control, shoving her hand out of the way and dipped his head between her legs.

"Oh…oh god…"

The tug of his mouth overwhelmed her, evoking unbearably hot sensations. His soft hair brushed feather-light over her pelvis as long fingers pried the folds apart, his tongue strumming across her aching clit. Alternating between sucking and sinuous licks, Tomas tormented the drenched flesh, slipping two thick fingers knuckles-deep and pumping in concert. Talia stared up at the ceiling, squirming helplessly but didn't dare dislodge his fingers as he rotated the digits in a circle and sampled the dewy wetness.

"Tomas, Tomas…" She chanted his name in a near-delirious state.

He grabbed her bottom with big hands and squeezed the plump flesh. The room spun and blurred at the relentless plunder of his mouth, and her whole body was seized by a brutal quivering in a desperate quest for release. He devoured her with such raw urgency, it was as if he'd been waiting for this moment and didn't want miss a single drop.

Eyes rolled back in her head, at the brink of a climax, Talia encouraged and begged in short, panting breaths, sinking her shaking fingers into the lushness of his hair. "Please. Yes, like that…*yes.*"

The orgasm was not subtle. It tore up her spine in a frenzy of explosions that left her gasping and shuddering. While her body still convulsed, he made love to her lower lips with his mouth, groaning his enjoyment—feasting like a man who'd finally been granted the one meal he craved.

Struggling to catch her breath, Talia twisted from his grasp and scooted back out of reach. She rolled onto her stomach and moaned into the mattress, inhaling whiffs of his scent from the sheets. She watched Tomas stand in slow motion, his passion-filled eyes glinting with satisfaction. He licked her honey from his lips and sent another tremor trickling through her at the sight.

A wicked grin tilted his lips upward. "Mmm…"

Her eyes followed him over to the wall where he flicked the switch and plunged the room in near-darkness. At the nightstand, he pulled a stack of foil packets from the top drawer and dropped them on the top.

"I think you're ready now," he said.

Talia ached to offer the same unselfish pleasure. "I want to touch you," she said.

She reached for him and wrapped her fingers around the distended staff between his legs. Tugging gently she pulled him closer, and a fierce fire lit his eyes when he joined her on the bed. Placing a leg on either side of his lap, she straddled his thick thighs. The tips of her fingers traced the bridge of his nose and over his mouth. He was an attractive man, even more so up close, and she marveled at the texture of his skin, how it was surprisingly soft and smooth. At the seam of his lips, she gently scraped the thumbnail over his skin, and he sucked her thumb in. That quickly, her loins flooded with heat as her body came alive again.

Her hair created a heavy curtain around them as she took her time dropping kisses on his eyelids and cheekbones. She feasted in much the same way he had consumed her, trailing her tongue over his shoulders, taking pleasure in the maleness of him and the spicy tang of his golden skin. His rough hands moved restlessly over her back, abrading with a sensual friction, sliding over the curve of her spine and caressing the swell of her derriere. A soft groan from him encouraged her to slide lower. She covered his chest and the sprinkling of hair with kisses, reveling in the involuntary jerk of his pecs when she flicked his flat nipples with her tongue.

Running her hands over his body, Talia was enamored by the abundance of muscle definition. Her touch lingered on his lean waist and she molded his hip with her palm. She massaged his abdomen and slid her hand over his pelvis, listening to the deep rumble in his chest as she moved to the tight muscles of his long legs.

She clasped his length in her hand, explored the veined exterior and stroked the broad tip. A drop of precum emerged from the slit in the end, and she rubbed the moisture over the head.

Tomas caught her wrist. "You're playing with fire," he said thickly.

She didn't hesitate, her heart racing with anticipation and a type of excitement she could never before remember feeling. "I want to get burned."

Talia eased down to lick the base of his shaft and laved the entire length. His salty taste coated her tongue, and with her hand on the base, she sucked the bulbous tip into her mouth.

Tomas's face contorted into a pleasure-filled grimace. He stared at his hard flesh sliding in and out of her mouth, between those full, luscious lips he'd fantasized about. "Talia," he groaned, gritting his teeth. He struggled not to thrust deep into the warm suction of her mouth, but she didn't make it easy when she took him deeper, sucking harder.

He inhaled sharply and sat up. "No," he said, though it was a difficult.

Confusion filled her eyes. "What's wrong? You didn't like it?"

"Oh yes. I liked it too much," he said with a shaky laugh. "But the first time I come, I want to be inside you. Come here." He pulled her up to him. "I want you to get on top of me. I want you to ride."

He grabbed one of the packets, settled against the pillows, and sheathed his erection. Positioned above him, Talia eased down and gasped when he breached her entrance. It had truly been a long time for her. She was so tight and hot, his upper lip twitched.

For one endless moment, they stared into each other's eyes. "Tomas...?" she whispered, a sound of alarm in her voice.

"Hold onto me," he instructed.

Her nails sank into his shoulders. "I—"

"I've got you, *querida*," he said thickly. He cupped her face, drawing her lips down to his. "I've got you," he whispered again before seizing her mouth. His hips shifted and he thrust upward. She gasped into his mouth. He stretched the tender muscles, filling the tight, wet cocoon. He groaned. She felt incredible, and being inside of her made him feel as if he hadn't been with a woman in ages. His hips rotated to hit every corner, and she began to moan from the pleasure of it.

He knew the moment she became lost in the sensations of their joined bodies. She sat up straighter and began an excruciatingly slow, erotic slide up and down on his shaft. His hands ran over her shapely thighs. He grabbed a handful of her soft hair and gently tugged to arch her throat. He kissed her there, tasting the sweetness of her skin, savoring the flavor.

He couldn't stop looking at her as she moaned, lips parted, breasts thrust forward as a delicious offering. He rolled her beneath him and bore down between her legs. Bodies crushed together, he plunged hard. The succulent chocolate fruit of her breasts, crowned with dark plum-colored berries, bounced with each jerk of his hips. He couldn't resist tugging one between his lips, suckling the puckered skin. The sound of her gasping cries were the sweetest sounds he'd ever heard.

Lengthening each stroke, he dived deeper and breathed words into her mouth in his native Spanish. "Talia, *t'eres tan bella. Mierda...deliciosa... querida...*"

Like talons, her manicured nails dug into his back. "So good, so good..." she whispered in an anguished voice.

He twisted with her in his arms again and rolled them to the edge of the bed. Her head hung over the side, her ebony mane reaching almost to the floor. His breathing came harsher, the sounds of her breathless cries consuming him. One hand gripped her supple ass and the other fastened lightly around her throat to hold her in place over the side of the bed. He pumped faster, hard as steel, burying inside the slippery heat.

Her eyes rolled back in her head and mouth

fell open. "Like that...give it to me...harder ...*please*."

She stared unseeing up at the ceiling, her vision foggy. Hanging upside down made the blood rush to her head, her brain fuddled as he held her down and thrust like a piston. Her heels dug into the mattress as she lifted her hips into his. "I'm coming," she whimpered. "I'm...coming!"

Talia reached for Tomas, clawing his shoulder and hanging on for dear life as blood rushed to her head and she was pushed over the edge. Her feminine muscles twitched and convulsed around his thickness. She let out a scream in a voice she would never have been able to identify as her own. And as the orgasm arrowed up her spine in a dark wave, it threw her body taut.

Seconds later, breathing hard, Tomas collapsed on top of her. He immediately rolled over and pulled her with him, and they lay wrapped in each other's arms until their breathing returned to normal.

"I'll be right back," he said softly.

Watching him go into the bathroom, Talia slipped under the sex-scented sheets. When he came back to the bed, he slid on top of her and kissed her neck. He was already hard again. A powerful erection nudged her thigh, and she didn't have the power to refuse.

She wrapped her limbs around him, feeling safe, warm, and desired. Ready for another round.

Chapter Eleven

Without opening her eyes, Talia knew she was in an unfamiliar place. Because of the sheets. They weren't the soft silk she was accustomed to in her king sized bed at home. Cotton?

Wait a minute, she didn't have any clothes on. She never slept naked. *What the…?*

Her eyes flew open and she struggled through the sleepy fog to re-orient herself. Squinting against the morning light coming in through the window, she stared at the unfamiliar surroundings. Unfamiliar dark dresser, unfamiliar photos of smiling people on the wall, unfamiliar king size bed. She didn't recognize the sounds outside, either, or rather the lack of sounds. No cars honked, doors slammed, or people yelled. All was quiet.

The man to her left was not unfamiliar, though.

The pale blue sheets wound around his waist

gave her a good view of his muscular back and the thick arms that had held her close for most of the night, proving she was still very much desirable. Sex with him had given her a morale boost, and he'd more than lived up to the rumors.

Throughout the night he allowed her to doze for short periods, recharge, and then he'd awaken her with kisses and heated caresses that roused her desire to a feverish pitch. She'd been surprised at her unquenchable hunger for him.

Talia rolled onto her side and ran her hand over her hair, lengthening her body into a much-needed stretch. Exhausted, she didn't want to get up. Last night had given her quite a workout, but she couldn't stay in bed all day.

She slipped from under the covers and padded over to where her underwear lay on the floor. As she stepped into it, she caught her reflection in the mirror over the dresser and grimaced. Rumpled hair and no makeup made her look like a hot mess. It had been a long, rough night. Her body ached in places she didn't even know had muscles, but she couldn't complain. She'd enjoyed every minute of it. The man had skills.

Her cheeks burned when she thought of all the things they'd done to each other. The way she'd explored his sculpted body and wrapped her limbs around him. His lips on her back, hips, and inner thigh. The way he'd licked every inch of skin, as if to embed the taste of her on his tongue.

She let out a soft sigh, on the verge of collapsing from the memory of all the pleasure she'd experienced. They'd made good use of the bed and the chair beside it. Her thigh muscles ached from having her legs twisted in pretzel-like formations, and she was pretty sure the pain in her lower back had been self-inflicted as she curled her spine to take more of his commanding strokes from behind. He'd set the bar ridiculously high for any man who came after him.

"What are you doing?" Tomas's husky voice filled the room, sounding even lower in the early morning and making her want to crawl back under the covers with him.

She turned in time to see him push his untamed hair back from his brow. He looked yummy as he stretched, with his disheveled hair and stubble covering his jaw. He folded his arms behind his head, a sexy, sleepy look clinging to his heavy-lidded eyes. Why hadn't she ever paid attention to him before? Oh yeah, she'd been married.

"Good morning."

Her own voice sounded hoarse and scratchy. Probably from all the screaming she'd done while under him. Thank goodness his closest neighbor lived a couple of miles away, but she wasn't completely certain they hadn't heard her, even from that distance.

She continued to get dressed.

"I guess you won't be joining me for breakfast?" Humor filled his voice.

"No, it's best I leave. I have a million things to do."

"It's Sunday."

Talia took a deep breath and pulled her strapless bra over her breasts before facing him again. She'd have to be direct. "Look, last night was wonderful. Thank you. Actually, it was just what I needed, but it won't happen again."

One dark brow shot up. The same amused expression remained on his face. "No?"

What was he smiling about? "No."

"*Qué lástima,*" he murmured.

He'd whispered all sorts of things in Spanish to her last night, most of which she didn't understand, but they had turned her on. She recognized that particular phrase, but again, she failed to recollect much of what she'd learned of the language in school.

"What does that mean?"

"What a pity," he said.

Silence fell over the room. His regretful tone set her heart to pounding at an accelerated pace. His gaze took a leisurely stroll over her covered breasts, down to her bare midriff and thighs. Any other man, any other situation, she would have been offended, but she was half-naked in his bedroom, and after all the ways they'd made love to each other, offended was the last thing she felt. Once again, the urge to crawl back under the covers with him overcame her. One night and she was already addicted to the man.

"It's nothing personal," she continued, in an effort to squash her rising libido.

"You got what you needed." He shrugged and yawned. "I like a woman who knows what she wants, and when she gets it can move on. If only more women were like you."

That hadn't been the response she'd expected.

He rose from the bed. Large feet and powerful

thighs took him across the room away from her. She watched the paler skin of his naked rear, admiring the firm, sinuous muscles of his glutes. Red lines criss-crossed his back where her nails had scored his skin. Her lips tingled with the desire to kiss those spots and soothe away the hurt. The same fine hairs on his chest were sprinkled down the length of his legs, and she gulped at the memory of his golden thighs sliding along the length of her darker flesh as he pried her legs apart.

Talia struggled to pay attention to his actions, but she finally registered he'd picked up her crumpled dress from the floor. He handed it over with an outstretched hand.

"Do you need any help getting dressed?" he asked. He sounded serious, but she knew he was kidding. He stood in front of her without a stitch of clothing on, making it incredibly hard to concentrate because she wanted to drop her gaze lower but was determined not to.

"No assistance needed."

She turned her back to him and stepped into the dress, shirking the feeling of disappointment that he'd easily accepted this as a onetime hookup and didn't have any problem with letting her leave. She hadn't expected anything more, but did he have to be so agreeable about it?

"Are you sure this won't ever happen again?" he whispered close behind her, so close his breath stirred the frizzy hairs on her head. He zipped the dress, the heat from his body touching hers. Before she could respond, two large hands came to rest on her waist.

His touch made her skin tingle, tempting her to answer in the negative, but in all honesty, she was in no condition to get involved with anyone right now. The breakup of her marriage was too fresh and raw. Rebounding with a man like Tomas would be enjoyable at first, but she knew it had the potential to become problematic. She was already fiending for him like a drug addict after one night. Clearly she couldn't handle anything complicated. Last night she'd received the boost she needed, and it would have to do.

"Yes, I'm positive it will never happen again."

Pulling away, Talia cleared her throat. "If you don't mind, I'd prefer no one found out about this."

He stilled and his face sobered. "Why not?"

She didn't know why not except their tryst was private and she didn't want him to cheapen what happened by bragging to Ryan or any of the other men in his circle about his latest conquest.

"I just don't."

"If that's what you want, no problem," he said evenly, but his face tightened as if he did have a problem with the request.

"Good, I'm glad we understand each other."

She smoothed her palm along the sides of her hair. From the corner of her eye she saw him drag on a pair of navy blue boxer briefs and sit on the edge of the bed.

"Should I feel used?" he asked.

"Of course not." His question surprised her.

"If I treated you the way you're treating me, you would be offended." The detached tone of voice conflicted with the hard set of his jaw, suggesting turbulent emotions brewing below the surface.

"Hardly. I'd be grateful you weren't making a big deal out of what happened last night."

"Of course. Because you're the ice princess."

"Don't call me that," Talia snapped, pausing to stare him down in the mirror.

She hated any word that implied she was anything but a warm person—cold, frosty, frigid. She'd heard them all and hated them all. Reluctant to examine the reason behind her reaction, she only knew that to have him—of all people—call her an ice princess made the painful barb cut even deeper.

"You're right, that is an unfair comment," he said with a measure of insolence. "Once you get warmed up, there's nothing cold about you. I could barely keep you off of me."

This wasn't his usual teasing. She could tell he was annoyed with her. Well, she wouldn't take his comments lying down and had a snide observation of her own.

"Excuse me?" She turned away from the mirror. "You're the one who couldn't wait to get me over here. You kept bringing it up and practically strong armed me."

"You stayed behind because I strong armed you?" he mocked.

"What's the matter, Tomas, are you mad because I haven't fallen all over you like your groupies? What do you want, a pat on the back? Okay, here goes—the sex was good."

"Good?" His jaw tensed. "Try spectacular, *querida*. Tell the truth."

Querida. He'd called her that all through the night, whispered it in her ear along with streams of Spanish words whose melodious sounds had been like music to her ears, keeping her hot, and desperate, and aching for him. Now he was making it ugly. Instead of the beautiful endearment it should be, he'd turned the word into a grotesque mockery without the same affection, the same passion, the same sensual promise.

Talia's eyes narrowed. "I knew it," she said. "I knew I shouldn't have slept with you. I let you coerce me into—"

He bolted from the bed and grabbed her so fast she never saw the move coming. His fingers sank into the soft flesh of her upper arm and his eyes flashed whiskey-colored flames. "Stop using the words coerce and strong-arm," he grated. "They give the impression I have to force a woman to have sex with me, and we both know that's not true. You got what you wanted, and I got what I wanted. Let's be adult about this, okay?"

When he released her, she stumbled back and rubbed the spot where he'd touched her.

"I don't like the way you talk about me, either. I'm not some desperate woman who needs..." She waved her hand expressively. "Whatever it is you think you have to offer."

"What I have to offer," he said, stalking forward to stand in her personal space, "is much more than what's between my legs. But I don't think I would even offer you that again. You don't deserve it."

"D-deserve it?" Talia sputtered. "You are an arrogant, narcissistic—" She broke off when he burst into laughter. "What are you laughing about?"

"Too bad we don't like each other," he said. "I think I would learn so many interesting words from you."

"Oh, I have plenty of interesting words I'd like for you to learn." Starting with a four-letter one.

"I'm certain I know those already. The first English words I learned were the bad ones."

He walked away from her with his usual cocky gait that this time made her livid. He headed toward the open door of the bathroom. "See yourself out," he said. "And don't leave anything behind as an excuse to come back. I know how you women are."

The door shut with finality behind him.

Talia stomped over and yelled, "You don't have to worry about me leaving anything behind. I never, *ever* want to see you again, and I certainly have no reason to come back out here to this hell hole."

When he didn't respond, she muttered a stream of profanity. With one last look around the room to ensure she left nothing behind, she hurried out so she wouldn't have to see him when he came back into the room.

Tomas left the bathroom as soon as he heard the bedroom door slam. Holding his toothbrush, he walked over to the window and braced one hand at the top of the sill. He watched Talia walk stiffly across the yard and climb into her gold Mercedes coupe, a car boasting leather trim and enough electronic gadgets to make Q of the James Bond films salivate. An image car whose characteristics matched those of its owner— exquisite and sleek.

The engine roared to life, and she drove down the dirt driveway toward the main road. He didn't move, even when the cloud of dust made visibility of the vehicle difficult. Her angry departure had not been the way he envisioned their day would begin. He'd hoped for a more pleasurable start to the morning. Sexual frustration roared through his body.

Nerve-wracking woman.

Bristling with anger, he slammed his fist into the wall.

Chapter Twelve

On Saturday Talia drove through Ryan and Shawna's quiet neighborhood. Today was the first time she'd been back to the house since the party.

An entire week had passed since her night with Tomas and she hadn't heard from him. Not that she'd expected to, it was just that...Her fingers gripped the steering wheel.

Why couldn't she forget him? She sympathized with all those women she'd previously thought of as foolish. No wonder he hid out in the country. She almost wanted to become a stalker herself.

She should've heeded Shawna's warning and not slept with him because he definitely knew what he was doing in the bedroom. How many times had she seen women lose their minds when they came into contact with a man like him? One who offered the kind of sex that made you do crazy things, like hand him the keys to your car or use words like "making love" when it was just sex—albeit of the mind-blowing, toe-curling variety.

Goodness, she had to pull it together or Shawna would see right through her and know something was wrong.

She turned left down the street to the cul-de-sac. Out here, the cars in the garages tended toward four door sedans and mini-vans. Most of the homes were filled with husbands and wives with a few kids, a dog, and maybe even a goldfish. A far cry from her loft in the Old Fourth Ward.

Children tossing a ball scampered out of her path so she could pull into the driveway. She let herself into the house.

"Hello! Where is everybody?" she called out.

"I'm in here," Shawna called back.

The inviting aroma of a home-cooked meal greeted her nose, and when she entered the kitchen she saw Shawna washing vegetables at the sink in the island. Near her feet, sitting on a red plastic mat, Ryker played with a collection of colorful plastic bowls and a wooden spoon. When Talia entered he looked up.

"Hey, handsome," she cooed.

She tickled his belly and he giggled, giving her one of his dimpled smiles and then went right back to pounding on the bowls.

"Are you okay?" Shawna asked. "You're not getting sick, are you? You look flushed."

"I'm fine." Talia waved off her comment. "I was riding with the car windows down," she lied. "Not a good idea in this heat."

"Pour yourself some water and cool off."

"Are those his latest toys?" Talia asked to

distract her friend's attention. Meanwhile she poured chilled water in a glass.

"I'm afraid so. He hardly touches any of the real toys we buy for him. He'd rather pull my pots and pans from the cabinet and bang them around, which makes way too much noise. I put latches on the lower cabinets, but he cried every time he couldn't get in, so I surrendered and let him have one of the shelves. I moved the plastic bowls and some of his toys down there for him to play with. At least they don't make as much noise as the pots and pans."

Talia went to the other side of the island. She sipped the water and felt her body temperature lower. Much better.

She peeped out the window. "I see Ryan finally put the swing set together."

Shawna laughed. "Ryker insisted on helping him, and I laughed my butt off watching those two. Ryan tried to stay calm while Ryker kept picking up bolts and screws and moving them around. I have a video of them. One day when you have time we'll watch it together. You'll get a good laugh."

Talia watched Shawna shift vegetables into the colander to drain. "You need any help?"

"No, I'm almost done."

The front door opened and the jingle of keys made Ryker look up from playing with the dishes. "Daddy!"

"Yes," Shawna said. "Daddy's home."

"Daddy! Daddy!" Ryker scrambled to his feet, his wide-legged unstable gait taking him as fast as he could out of the kitchen.

"How long has Ryan been gone? It's only been since this morning, right? He acts like he hasn't seen him in years."

"I think kids are like that in general. They're always excited to see the parent they spend the least amount of time with."

Ryan walked in with his son hanging upside down by one leg, squealing and laughing.

"Hi, baby," Shawna said in a softened voice.

"Hey, love." Holding his son with one hand, Ryan pulled Shawna closer with the other and kissed her lightly on the mouth. Then he kissed her cheek and nuzzled her neck. "Mmm…you smell good."

"Like fried chicken?"

"Mmmhmm. And macaroni and cheese." He tickled Ryker and the little boy giggled and squirmed, still upside down.

"If you drop my son," Shawna warned.

"He'll be all right." Ryan grinned at Talia. "A fall on the head will toughen him up."

"Ha-ha. Dinner's almost ready. Go get washed up, and take your son with you."

Shawna dipped a baby carrot in dressing and placed it in Ryan's mouth. Their perfectly choreographed routine must have played out a thousand times before, their affectionate behavior illustrating their love for each other. Considering the rocky start to their relationship, Talia couldn't be happier for them. After a brief encounter that ended disastrously years ago in Chicago, by chance, Ryan and Shawna ended up in Atlanta at different times. After orchestrating a blind date with her, Ryan managed to win her back.

Had she ever had such an intense love for Carter, or he for her? Had they ever had this sort of easy familiarity, where one anticipated the other's actions and knew the other's thoughts without uttering a word? She couldn't remember, but every time she saw her friends together, she longed for that type of relationship. All their happiness and domestic bliss made it hard not to feel jealous.

"You staying for dinner, Talia?" Ryan called as he walked to the half bath in the hallway.

"No, I just stopped in to say hi."

She heard the front door open again. "¡*Hola!*" a male voice called.

Talia stilled.

No, not him.

Ignoring the betraying acceleration of her pulse, she stood up straight, tossed back her shoulders and prepared to give Tomas the cold shoulder. When he appeared in the doorway, she couldn't help but catch her breath. The gray T-shirt he wore clung to his abs and defined chest, and the worn jeans brought attention to his long legs. Damn, he looked good.

His eyes drifted over her. "Talia," he said. His voice held no emotion.

She schooled her face into a cool expression, about to greet him in the same emotionless way when a woman appeared behind him and the words lodged in her throat.

"Hi, Tomas," Shawna greeted him. "Hi, Bianca. How are you?"

Bianca, a tall, svelte Hispanic woman, wore a pair of jeans leaving nothing to the imagination.

They fit over her ample hips and long legs like a second skin. Her pouty red lips lifted into a friendly smile when she saw Talia.

"Bianca, this is one of my best friends, Talia," Shawna said. "Talia, this is Bianca. She's a friend of Tomas's."

"I'm a good, good friend of Tomas." Bianca spoke with a thick Spanish accent. She stuck out her hand. "Nice to meet you."

"Likewise," Talia said, clasping her hand firmly and pumping hard.

She glanced at Tomas and quickly turned away from his searching eyes. Fighting back the jealousy that bubbled to life inside her, she concentrated on the glass in front of her as if the secrets of the universe lay hidden in the water. She certainly didn't own him and had insisted their night together was a onetime occurrence, but she hadn't expected this. Not so soon. A prick of pain sprouted in her chest. It hurt a little. It hurt a lot. There she'd been, thinking about him, aching for him, and he'd already moved on.

Ryan came out of the bathroom and Ryker ran ahead of him. He ran around Bianca and latched onto Talia's leg.

"Hey, little man," she murmured, scooping him up in her arms. "You want to play with me now, huh?"

"Be careful," Ryan warned. "You know he's a breast man."

Sure enough, Ryker patted Talia's chest and then rested his head on her cleavage.

"Ryker!" Shawna scolded, doing her best to hide a smile but failing miserably.

His head popped up, as if to check if his mother was really angry. Then he broke out into a big smile that could spread sunshine on a rainy day. He burst into a fit of giggles, making the adorable sound children make when they're being mischievous, and then he plopped his head back onto Talia's chest.

"I told you he knows exactly what he's doing," Shawna said to Ryan.

"That's my boy!" Ryan said, and pumped his fist.

Shawna elbowed him in the ribs, and he dragged her close with a laugh, planting a loud kiss on her neck.

"He's okay," Talia said, rubbing circles on Ryker's back and swaying from side to side with him in her arms. She kissed the top of his head.

This might be the closest she ever came to having a child. She'd decided a baby wasn't in her future because she had to concentrate on her career. Yet her chest ached, and she battled the deluge of sadness that always buffeted her insides when she thought of never having children of her own.

She hid her face in Ryker's neck and relished the moment. She closed her eyes, temporarily transported from the kitchen and inhaled powder and his clean baby smell.

Maybe later she could have a baby, if there was time.

Ryker squirmed to get down and ran over to where his father was taking out plates and silverware to set the table.

"I'd like to wash up before dinner," Bianca said. "Where's the bathroom?"

Shawna pointed with a stalk of celery. "Turn there. First door on your right."

As Bianca exited, Tomas came to stand beside Talia, brushing against her. Having no doubt he'd done it on purpose, she stepped aside. "Are you staying for dinner?" he asked in a low voice.

"No." She wouldn't look at him, keeping her eyes on Ryan and Ryker's interaction. Ryan handed a spoon to his son so he could participate in getting the table ready for dinner.

"Don't leave on my account."

"I'm not doing anything on your account."

"I know how this looks, but she's a friend."

"A good, good friend," Talia said snidely. She sounded like a jealous hag, unable to curb the bitterness that crept into her voice. Would it be wrong to scratch out Bianca's eyes?

"My friend Manny owns a Cuban restaurant where I hang out a lot, and she's his cousin," Tomas explained. "She's new to Atlanta and I'm being friendly by introducing her to people and showing her around."

"That's very nice of you, but you don't have to explain anything to me. By the way, does being friendly include having sex with her?" She held her breath.

"I'm not having sex with her," he said evenly.

She didn't let on how much his response thrilled her. "Will wonders never cease? You can actually exercise restraint," she said from the corner of her mouth.

They spoke in low tones so Ryan and Shawna, preoccupied with each other and Ryker, couldn't hear.

He leaned closer, and his warm breath brushed her ear when he spoke. "Why are you so mean, hmm? Am I going to have to put you over my knee and spank that cute little ass of yours again, *pequeña?*"

Talia drew in a sharp, silent breath and closed her eyes briefly.

The vivid memory of how he'd paddled her bare bottom with his hand, each blow stinging and arousing at the same time, came back with brutal force. She'd experienced an incredible orgasm—her first from that kind of contact. Then when he'd finished he put her on the bed and soothed her throbbing skin with moist kisses. She'd thought he'd stop there, but then he'd pushed her thighs apart and licked at the moisture between her legs, using one hand in the middle of her back to hold her face down until his tongue had wrenched another orgasm from her.

She moistened her lips, acutely aware of how his words alone had affected her body. Thanks to him, she now throbbed and ached at a most inopportune time.

"Shawna, I'm leaving," she said loudly.

"Oh." Disappointment filled Shawna's voice. "You sure? There's plenty of food."

"Yes, I'm sure." Talia grabbed for her keys on the marble countertop but accidentally knocked them to the floor. Tomas picked them up.

"Here you go."

Instead of dropping them into her hand, he placed them in her palm and purposely raked his calloused fingers across her skin, extending contact between them longer than necessary and reminding her of how his rough hands had caressed her entire body with commendable single-mindedness. Tingles darted across her skin, and from the laughter in his eyes, he knew exactly the effect he was having on her.

She clamped her hand around the keys and fixed Tomas with the dirtiest look she could muster. "See you guys later."

She hurried out of the house, raced down the steps to her car, and sped out of the subdivision with the swiftness of a drag racer. Berating herself, she insisted she was every kind of fool for wanting a man so obviously callous in his relationships. But no amount of self-rebuke could hide the truth—how difficult it would be to ignore him when he'd made such an indelible mark on her mind and body.

Not when her heart was thudding. Her blood pounding. And her panties wet.

Chapter Thirteen

Call him.
No!

Talia twirled in her office chair. The same argument rewound in her head all day. Since she'd left Tomas's house, she hadn't been able to find her Prada sunglasses, and she wanted to call and ask if he'd found them, but knowing him he'd think she'd purposely left them there as an excuse to get back in touch.

Groaning, she buried her head in her hands. *Enough already!*

She had work to do and had skipped lunch to prepare for a meeting with Jay and others on the executive team but hadn't made much headway. If she grabbed a snack from the vending machine, she could appease her empty stomach and spend the next thirty minutes or so preparing for the meeting.

She rose from the chair and walked across her

office, running through the checklist of items she had to complete before the end of the day. She opened the door but pulled up short when she saw Tomas standing on the other side, smiling and talking to her secretary at her desk. Their cozy little tête-à-tête fueled her anger at him.

"What are you doing here?"

Lillian jumped guiltily to her feet. "I was about to call and let you know you have a visitor."

Talia's lips tightened and she folded her arms over her chest. "I said, what are you doing here?"

She shot daggers at Tomas and knew she was being a bitch, but damn him for looking so delicious without even trying, with a rough ponytail, wearing a pair of distressed jeans and another T-shirt that he knew good and well was too small when he bought it. No other man she knew managed to look so good with such little effort.

"I came to talk to you, if it's not too much to ask," he said.

She wanted to slap the smirk off his face.

"About what?"

"Would you like me to discuss it in front of Lillian?"

The way he said her secretary's name sounded intimate, as if they'd known each other for a long time. Her gaze bounced between them, noting Lillian's flushed cheeks and how she couldn't meet her gaze.

"Hold my calls."

Talia stalked back into her office and expected him to follow, but of course he did so on his own time. She could hear him outside talking to Lillian in a low voice and they laughed again, infuriating her more. He finally came in, shut the door, and walked over to her desk like he had nowhere to go and nothing to do and expected the same of her.

"So this is where you work." He surveyed the room.

"Make it fast. I have a lot of work to do." She sat down and crossed her legs.

He reached into the pocket of his jeans and pulled out a pair of sunglasses. Her sunglasses. Holding them up, he asked, "Look familiar?"

She straightened in the chair. "Where did you find them?"

"Where you put them, under the table in the kitchen."

"I did not put them there. They must have fallen out of my purse when I put it on the table."

He smirked. "Come on, Talia."

She sighed in defeat. He thought exactly what she'd imagined. "What's the point? Believe whatever you want."

He set down the glasses and walked around the desk to perch his firm backside right in front of her. The arrogance! Who else would do such a thing? Who else would have the audacity to sit on the edge of her desk as if it was his office? Not to mention sitting there brought him too close for comfort. He didn't comprehend the concept of personal space and the etiquette of boundaries.

She stared at the wall behind him.

"Why are you so upset?" he asked.

"I'm not," she said coldly.

"Yes, you are. If you didn't leave them behind

on purpose, you should be happy I found your overpriced sunglasses."

She made the grave mistake of looking up at him, intending to inform him her sunglasses were not overpriced and quality was worth the cost, but the words lodged in her throat. He was watching her legs, covered in sheer black stockings. Well, he could look all he wanted, because he'd never get another chance to—

He licked his lips, and her breath stuttered. His gaze now rested on the rise and fall of her chest. The acute interest made her realize how labored her breathing had become, and her traitorous nipples swelled in anticipation.

"Are you upset because of Bianca?" he asked.

"I don't care about you and your little escapades," she said with a flippant wave of her hand.

"Are you sure? Because you're pretty mad for someone who doesn't care." His voice sounded low and as smooth as silk.

"You need to get out of my office."

"Tell the truth, you don't want me to go."

She rose from the chair. "I'll escort you out."

Before she could get around him, he caught her by the waist and twirled her around, pulling her between his open legs. She brought up her hands to resist being crushed against his hard chest.

"I admit it," he said in a low voice. "You win."

"What are you talking about?" she whispered, already breathless.

"I was glad when I found the planted sunglasses because I wanted to see you again."

He brushed his lips to her chin. The barely there touch was deliciously erotic.

"I didn't...plant them," she panted, silently cheering that he'd wanted to see her. She could barely concentrate while he nibbled on her neck. Her swollen nipples became hard nubs and wet heat flooded the apex of her thighs.

"No?" He licked the spot where her shoulder and neck met.

"No," she insisted, leaning into his tongue. His big hands palmed her bottom and pulled her snug into his body.

"Do you still want me to leave?"

"Yes. No. I..."

"*Me gusta como hueles,*" he whispered. "What scent is that?"

"It's...um...I think it's..."

Her mind went blank when he squeezed her bottom. These same hands had restrained her passionate responses and soothingly caressed her damp skin after their marathon session in his bed almost put her in an orgasm-induced coma. She simply couldn't concentrate.

His mouth fused to hers, prying her lips apart for an intimate tangling of tongues. He plundered the deep recesses of her mouth, and the kiss deepened, becoming almost violent. Her nails dug into his tight shoulders, and the next thing she knew, he'd lifted her from the floor and deposited her on the desk. His hand slid up to the apex of her thighs, and one long finger stroked her clit through her panties.

"*Te desiro ahora. Aqui,*" he groaned.

She almost agreed. Right here, right now—

anything to quench the thirst for him she couldn't shake. But when he eased her backward, the prod of a stapler in her lower spine caused common sense to return.

"No, no, wait." She pushed at his chest. "We can't. This is where I work."

Heavy breaths fanned her face as he wrestled to regain control. Reluctantly she pushed his hand from between her legs and wiggled to a sitting position.

"You're right, this isn't a good idea," he said tersely, running his hand over his hair. "If it was after hours and we were here alone, maybe, but we both know you can be very...vocal."

"Excuse me?"

"That means loud. It means——"

"I know what it means," Talia said hotly, her cheeks burning.

A muscle in his jaw worked and his eyes devoured her as if he planned to rip the clothes right off her body and to hell with where they were. "When?"

"You want me to pick a time?"

"Yes."

He was serious, and she couldn't believe she was doing this. She shouldn't. "I don't know. Maybe later tonight, or——"

He moved closer, within inches until the heat from him warmed her already hot skin. "Let's go somewhere now."

Tempting offer—oh, so tempting. The impatience in his voice stoked the flames of her own desire. "If you're suggesting I leave work, I can't."

He was about to speak when a knock sounded on the door. She pushed him away and jumped off the desk right as Jay poked his head in. "Hi there, I didn't know if you were in or not. Lillian's not at her desk."

He came in, followed by Carter. Tomas stiffened, and Carter didn't look pleased to see him, either.

"Can I help you with something?" Talia asked, happy her voice sounded cool and professional instead of the breathless and needy quality from a few moments ago. She smoothed a hand down either side of her skirt.

When she noticed Jay's curious eyes land on Tomas, she introduced the men to each other. Tomas greeted Jay, but Carter stuffed his hands in his pockets and ignored Tomas.

Jay silently observed the dynamics in the room before he proceeded. "The meeting's been moved up because I need to leave early. I'll see you in fifteen minutes?"

Nowhere near ready, she'd have to throw something together. "Sure, that would be fine."

"Nice to meet you, Tomas."

"Nice to meet you, too." As soon as the two men left, Tomas turned to her. "Fifteen minutes doesn't give us much time."

Talia's eyes widened in disbelief at his insistence. "No way."

"Why not?"

"Because I have work to do." She pointed at the door. "You have to leave."

"You're sure?"

"Yes."

He stared at her, as if he could wear her down through telepathy. Finally he seemed to get the message and ran his hand over his face with a heavy sigh. "This isn't over." He walked toward the door.

"How about after work?" Talia blurted. She bit her lip.

He paused with his hand on the door and assessed her in silence. "I'll come by your place," he offered. "Six-thirty?"

"All right."

They made the arrangement like two people getting together to hang out. But already her hands became clammy as she looked forward to the prospect of seeing him later. She gave him the address, the entire time thinking she must have lost her mind. After he left, she sank into her chair. They weren't supposed to see each other again, but she'd just made an appointment to have sex. Yes, she was definitely losing her mind.

"Okay, what do I need to mention in the update?" Time to focus on work. On the top sheet of the legal pad on her desk, she wrote "JBC meeting" on the first line. She wrote a few words about the magazine ads, the color schemes, and the feedback she'd received from the Johnsons, every now and again tapping the pen against her mouth.

A few minutes later, the telephone on her desk rang, disturbing her concentration.

"Hello?"

"I couldn't wait." It was Tomas.

She held her breath and almost melted into the chair. "How'd you get my direct line?"

"Lillian was helpful earlier. Did you hear what I said?"

"Yes, I heard you, but what do you mean you couldn't wait?"

"I want you now."

She couldn't do this. Wouldn't. "I told you, I can't. I have to work."

"Meet me in the stairwell two floors below you."

She closed her eyes, fighting the temptation to give in. The grip on the pen in her hand tightened. "Tomas, the stairwell is just as inappropriate as my office."

"When you come, make sure you're not wearing any panties."

Her breathing fractured. "I'm not coming," she insisted, her voice smaller and less convincing.

"You have five minutes, and then I'm leaving."

"I have a meeting in ten minutes," she said.

"Don't be late." He wasn't even listening to her. Or he chose to ignore every word she said.

"If you think—" The line went dead.

Talia slammed down the phone. He was going to feel very foolish waiting down there when she didn't show up.

"Okay, where was I?" She twirled the pen in the corner of her mouth.

The second hand of the clock on her desk moved. A minute had passed.

She shifted in her seat and gnawed on the pen cap, concentration focused on the sheet in front of her. An idea came to her for the JBC campaign and she scribbled it down.

From the corner of her eye, she saw another minute pass.

She crossed one leg over the other and bounced her foot.

Another minute.

Exasperated, Talia turned the clock face away from her. She didn't need to see every single minute go by. The movement distracted her from the important task she had to complete.

Taking a deep breath, she drew a circle around an important point and wrote a few words in the corner, but right after, she dropped the pen on the desk and placed her head in her hands.

This was madness.

Before she changed her mind, she reached under her skirt and wriggled out of her thong. Dropping it into the bottom drawer, she gave herself a scolding for what she considered doing.

Shawna's words from the day of the picnic came back to haunt her. *He gets women to do all kinds of crazy things. They simply forget who they are.*

Pushing away the thought, she twisted the clock around. Five minutes had passed since he called, and he'd given her five to get down there. She sprang from the chair and rushed out the door to the exit at the end of the hallway. Gripping the handrail, she raced down the first flight of stairs, her high heels echoing loudly in the cavernous space. Heart racing, she hurried down the second set. Her ankle twisted and she lost a shoe but kept moving in a graceless hobble, hoping she hadn't missed him, wishing she hadn't been so stubborn in the first place when she wanted what he did.

Almost to the bottom step she came to an abrupt halt. He stood off to the right on the landing below, back to the wall, thumbs hooked in the loops of his jeans. One corner of his mouth lifted and his eyes crinkled in the corners. He knew she'd come.

"*Ven acá, pequeña.*"

She tried to gather some semblance of resistance, but her pride took a back seat to desire. She slipped off the other shoe and walked on the cold floor until she stopped right in front of him as he'd instructed.

"You're late," he said.

"I don't know why I'm here. I don't even like you," she said.

His lips twisted into a sexy, panty-wetting smile. "You don't have to like me to enjoy this."

He put his hand to the back of her neck and dragged her to him.

Chapter Fourteen

Tomas slid his hand up Talia's skirt. "*Dios*," he hissed. She had really removed her panties. His brain ceased to function and his penis started calling the shots.

Dragging the skirt past her hips, he exposed the black lace-edged garter on her silky thighs. In one controlled movement he lifted her from the floor and turned her against the wall.

One of her arms wound around his neck while the other reached between them. His stomach clenched at the scent of rosemary and mint in her hair. Night after night he'd jacked off to the same smell, tortured until he'd had to change the sheets.

She was the most frustrating woman he had ever met, and he couldn't get her out of his mind. He had no problem admitting the attraction between them, but even though she wanted him just as much, she chose to fight the fire between them.

He'd see about that.

His lips found her neck, and he applied his teeth and tongue to her skin, growing more excited with each breathless moan she made. She stroked him, and he lengthened and hardened with body-aching quickness until his jeans stretched uncomfortably over his groin.

"Take it out," he said in a tight voice.

She fumbled with the zipper as he sucked on her neck. He sucked hard, wanting to leave a mark the way she'd left marks on his back. He wanted her ex-husband to see. Wanted him to know if he entertained the notion they could get back together, he didn't stand a chance, though he had the privilege of seeing her every day at work. She belonged to him now.

He'd had a taste and now couldn't get enough. He wanted her all to himself. To think Ryan had warned him away. Ha. Someone should have warned him about her.

He pushed into her with a low growl, and his knees almost gave way. Wet and hot, she had him all confused and feeling helpless. With no will, no power, and solely at her mercy. His confidence wavered as the lines blurred and he was no longer certain who belonged to whom.

"Call me *papi*," he said in her ear.

"*Papi*," she whispered, sounding almost shy.

"Louder." He thrust harder, determined she would not walk away so easily this time. Not when this need for her wouldn't go away. Not when he couldn't forget, forced to recall their passionate romp every time he took a shower because soap stung the nicks left by her fingernails in his back.

"*Papi.*" Her voice shook, and her legs tightened around his lean hips.

"Louder." He went at her, thrusting deep, punishing her for depriving him.

"Oh, *papi,*" she gasped. "Oh, yes, so good. Yes, *papi.* Yes!"

Talia fisted her hands in his hair, pulling strands from the confines of the elastic ponytail holder, biting his neck, mouth open wide as she moaned, letting his pounding thrusts push her through to the inevitable climax.

Making love to him was so carnal, so out-of-control decadent. No one should enjoy sex this much. This kind of passion burned everything in its path. It almost felt wrong, this type of demanding. This type of taking. This type of glorious, heavenly fucking.

She locked harder around him and let loose a trembling cry when an orgasm tore through her. He continued to pound into her like a madman, his harsh breath fanning the side of her neck. The rhythm of his hips wrested yet another orgasm from her, and she cried out again, her voice bouncing off the stairwell walls, drowning his heavy grunts as he shuddered through a consuming climax. She only hoped she'd made it half as good for him as he made it for her.

They held each other tight afterward, their ragged breaths coming short and fast. Only when her heartbeat had slowed to an almost normal pace did he lower her to the ground and rest his head on the wall beside hers. With trembling fingers, Talia pulled her skirt back into place.

Tomas cleared his throat and zipped his jeans. "Next time, don't be late."

Next time?

"There will be a next time," he said.

He kissed the side of her mouth and helplessly, she let the tip of her tongue dip out to taste him. He sucked her lower lip and she whimpered.

"I'll be in touch," he said before heading down the stairs.

Talia remained in the stairwell and placed a hand over her chest to calm the erratic beat of her heart. She didn't know how to control this fire between them. It was out of hand. And she already wanted more—was looking forward to the *next time*, as he'd promised.

With a deep sigh she picked up the first abandoned shoe and started the slow climb up the stairs on shaky legs. She couldn't go to the meeting right away and would have to make a detour to the bathroom to fix her makeup and hair.

By the time she arrived in the boardroom she should have thought of a decent excuse to give Jay for being late.

Chapter Fifteen

The sun had gone down hours earlier, and the only light in the room came from a lamp on the nightstand. Talia stretched lazily in the bed. Another good workout, courtesy of Tomas Molina.

The dusting of hairs on his rock-hard chest tickled when he pressed against her back. Raining tender kisses onto her shoulder, he cupped a breast and pulled on the nipple. It hardened into a tight peak and desire unfurled again in her loins.

"We just had sex," she said, giggling. He had quite the libido, with such a short recovery time she sometimes doubted he'd lost his erection.

"These breasts drive me crazy," he complained. He kneaded the soft mound, his calloused palm creating a sensual friction. "I don't think I've ever enjoyed sucking a woman's breasts as much as I do yours."

Her lids lowered, savoring the words as

moisture pooled between her legs. He always said erotic things like that. Words that complimented the richness of her skin tone, lauded her curves, and flattered features that used to make her feel self-conscious. Used to, because a woman would have to be a fool not to appreciate the uniqueness of her own body when a man showed such constant appreciation of it.

He rolled her onto her back and pulled a hard nipple into his mouth. Prying her legs apart, his hot manhood pressed into her heat. She arched her back, gasping when his muscular thighs widened and spread her legs so he could go deeper. Running her fingers over his sweat-slick back, she caressed the contours and grooves of hard muscle. She absorbed the textures of him, the sinewy strength under her fingertips, the soft silk of his hair.

The pull of his mouth and the slow roll of his hips worked in tandem to bring her to a quick, shuddering climax. Fingernails dug into his shoulders and she let loose a soft cry. Her knees clenched around his naked hips, and he came with a harsh groan of male satisfaction before collapsing beside her.

Talia listened to the steady sound of his breathing, amazed at how her life had changed in such a short time. Since the day in the stairwell, their relationship had progressed quickly, and she'd become accustomed to this endless banquet of pleasure.

They'd started out meeting one or two days out of the work week. Tomas would hang around in town, and she'd call him when she left work.

Then they'd meet at her condo for wild, bone-melting sex. But it wasn't enough, and the number of days increased to include every Saturday, at which time she'd drive the hour to his house in the country, spend the night, and drive back on Sunday.

At first they only cared about scratching the itch for each other that wouldn't go away, but at some point even a couple of days per week proved insufficient, and their meetings became more than sexual. Eventually she gave him a key so when he left work he could stay at her place until she came home. She knew he was just as lost as she about how to handle the magnetic pull they had on each other.

"Are you hungry?" she asked, sitting up. "I could order some food."

"Sure. What did you have in mind?" He yawned, big and loud.

"I'm not sure. I'll decide when I see the menus."

They dragged out of bed. She threw on a blue silk robe, and he pulled on his jeans. Downstairs in the kitchen, Talia opened the drawer filled with menus, and Tomas started opening the cabinet doors.

What's he doing?

She watched him in silence. The only items on the shelves were her favorite items to snack on—gourmet cheese straws, creamy white nougat imported from France, chocolate chip cookies from the neighborhood bakery, and figs hand-dipped in dark chocolate and imported from Valencia, Spain.

"Do you have anything we can eat now, while we wait?" he asked.

Most of the time they walked to one of the restaurants near her condo. Years ago the area where she lived used to be crime-infested, but investors had swooped in and bought the properties. After fixing them up, young, affluent 20- and 30-somethings moved in. A testament to the changes, trendy cafes and restaurants sprouted up to accommodate that demographic with expensive coffee mixes and eclectic dining choices.

"What I have to eat is what you see," she said.

Continuing the search, Tomas opened the refrigerator, which contained nothing but water and juice. The only other items were her smoothie packets of diced fruit—quart-sized bags in the freezer containing bananas, strawberries, or whatever fruits and vegetables she'd picked up at the supermarket, so she'd only have to dump everything into a blender and add juice or water for a quick breakfast.

"Don't you ever cook?" he asked, closing the refrigerator. "You don't have anything. Not even eggs to whip up a basic omelet. We'll have to change that."

"I have no intention of changing anything," Talia said, bumping him with her hip. "I told you, growing up we had servants who took care of the day-to-day, so I never had to learn." She shrugged. "I don't clean, either. That's what the cleaning service is for. This isn't the Dark Ages."

"There's nothing wrong with cooking a man a meal."

"Nothing wrong with not cooking, either. Are your hands broken? Cook for yourself." Talia set one of the menus on the counter and flipped it open.

"I do cook for myself. It's cheaper and more convenient."

He bent close to her ear and placed both hands, palms down, on the counter in front of her. Goose bumps sprang up on the back of her neck, and her nipples pushed against the lining of the robe. He liked to get close to her, and when she didn't wear heels and he tipped his head down, it truly made her feel small—*pequeña* or "little one"—as he called her.

"I think the right man could have you barefoot, pregnant, and in the kitchen making pancakes," he said in a confident voice. Almost as if he thought he was that man.

She laughed at the thought of her making pancakes. She'd never made them. "Then you have nothing to worry about, because you are not the right man," she quipped.

He laughed and swatted her on the behind.

"Ow," Talia said, though it didn't hurt.

"Order me whatever you order for yourself, but add extra sides," he said on his way out the kitchen. "I'm going to take a shower."

"When you eat that much then I'm the one stuck having to help you burn off all those extra calories," she called out, smiling to herself.

"As if you mind," he called back.

****

Flat on his back on Talia's bed, Tomas stared up at the ceiling.

"Are you almost ready?" he called for the third time.

They were on their way to a *quinceañera* party for one of his friend's daughters. Well, they would be on their way if she ever came out of the bathroom. He'd arrived thirty minutes ago to pick her up, dressed and ready to go in a black jacket and white shirt. He'd been waiting ever since.

"Would you be patient!" she hollered back. "It takes time to look as good as I do every day."

And she called him arrogant.

The light in the bathroom extinguished and Tomas sat up. Talia came out wearing a gray, sequined cocktail dress, loose on top, but the fitted skirt clung to her round hips and bottom. She'd styled her hair in a lustrous array of curls piled on top of her head.

"What do you think?" she asked, placing her hands on her hips.

"*Muy bonita.*"

"Really?"

One corner of his mouth lifted into an indulgent smile. She preened under his gaze, dark brown eyes lighting up the way they always did whenever he paid her a compliment. He never grew tired of that expression in her eyes.

"Stop fishing for compliments and let's go." He still teased her whenever the urge hit him.

Talia slapped his arm. "I'm not fishing," she said tartly.

Later, they sat at a table with two other couples in a banquet hall filled with friends and family members of the birthday girl.

"I had no idea these *quinceañera* parties were

so extravagant," Talia whispered.

The catered dinner, a chocolate fountain, and a five-tier cake represented only part of the elaborate setup. Selena, the birthday girl, had arrived wearing a pastel-blue princess dress with her escort and twelve-member court. The stretch Hummer dropped them off in front of the banquet hall before they made their grand entrance.

A live band playing a mix of pop music and traditional Latin sounds had half the guests dancing. Vases in the middle of each table contained flowers in soft-hued colors—pastel blue, muted green, cream, and rose.

Tomas nodded. "The parties are an important rite of passage and represent the transition from being a girl to becoming a woman, but I think the tradition has lost some of its meaning as each family tries to outdo the other. I've known families to go into deep debt if they didn't have friends and family members to help offset the cost. Selena's mother, Maria, grew up poor and her parents couldn't afford a nice party, so she wanted to make Selena's *quinces* special and memorable."

"Seeing her dance the first dance with her father was very sweet," Talia said quietly.

A wistfulness filled her voice and he saw the longing in her eyes. It was near the end of summer and they'd been together for several months, but he didn't know much about her parents except that her father had died when she was an infant and her mother had died during childbirth. She seldom talked about either of them.

Tomas put his arm around her shoulders, prompted by a sudden need to protect and comfort. "They practiced the waltz for weeks."

"They looked good out there," Talia said.

Tomas explained the symbolism of the other events at the party. "Remember when Selena changed from wearing the flats to the heels and received the last doll?" Talia nodded. "They symbolize her maturity now that she's a woman."

He ate the last piece of cake on his plate, and sensed Talia's gaze on him. The adoration in her eyes made his chest swell. She made him feel that way quite often—proud, as if he were some kind of hero.

"I'm glad you brought me. Thank you for sharing your culture with me," she said softly.

If anyone had told him three months ago he'd be at a party with Talia Jackson and lucky enough to be sharing her bed, he'd think they were crazy. He'd always been attracted to her, he realized, but she'd been married, untouchable. All the friendly animosity between them he now had to admit was nothing more than unacknowledged sexual tension.

She'd started doing thoughtful little things for him lately, like creating special smoothie packets that combined flavors she thought he'd enjoy— mango, papaya, and coconut milk. One smoothie she called the muscle builder, which included protein powder, and another packed with raspberries and bananas she said was good for his heart. His heart. Other women only seemed concerned about the organ between his legs.

She placed her soft hand at the back of his

neck and applied pressure, lifting her lips. Their mouths met in a slow, gentle kiss.

"What was that for?" he asked.

"Do I need a reason?"

Something inside him stirred. A faint, peculiar emotion that made him want more. Permanence. Monogamy. Those words used to scare him but had a more attractive ring to them now.

He and Talia had grown close, and he'd shared details with her about his life that he'd never shared with anyone. He'd told her about his childhood in Cuba and the devastation of losing his father in a boating accident at the age of nine. His poor upbringing presented a striking contrast to hers. While his family had relied on barter and government rations to supply their needs, she'd never had to ask the cost of anything because price didn't matter. He grew up in a small house with his brothers, mother, a cousin, and his grandparents. She grew up in a mansion with a nanny, servants, and the only other family member, her grandmother.

Manny, his Cuban friend who owned the restaurant, shuffled over. He had a slight limp from a bone fracture that never properly set when he was a child.

"We're going over to the restaurant afterward," he said. "Are the two of you coming?"

"Is the band playing tonight?" Tomas asked.

"Sure is. Food and drinks on me."

"Food?" Talia interjected. "After all this, you plan to eat again?"

"Trust me, you'll be ready to eat again once you get through with all the dancing." Manny winked. "See you two there." He ambled away.

"You want to go?" Tomas asked.

She nodded vigorously. "Of course. Sounds like fun."

Sometimes, when she reacted so happily to one of his suggestions that they go out with his friends, he wondered what her life had been like before. And why he hadn't met more of her friends. Outside of Shawna and Ryan, initially bewildered but now wholeheartedly accepting of their relationship, he didn't know anyone else close to her. Not friends and not family, either.

She seemed to have a strange relationship with her grandmother, a woman she seldom talked about but who could influence a change in mood with only a phone call. On those days his only goal was to make her happy and lose the pinched expression she wore after one of their conversations.

"We'll stay a little longer, say goodbye, and then leave for the restaurant," he said.

Chapter Sixteen

The patio of Tío Manny's Restaurant overflowed with a boisterous group of diners when Talia and Tomas arrived. A five-piece band rocked out a vaguely familiar Spanish tune, one she'd probably heard Tomas listening to in the car. The electric guitar player hunched over her instrument, face scrunched into concentrated lines while customers stood on their feet clapping and cheering.

Manny waved them over and introductions were made. Of the nine people at the table, Talia recognized four from the birthday party.

In addition to pitchers of margaritas, everyone had their own drink—*mojitos*, *Cuba Libres*, and for the less adventurous, good old Georgia sweet tea.

The waitress came over. "What can I get you two to drink?"

"A *Cuba Libre* for me, and a *piña colada* for her," Tomas replied.

Manny shouted across the table to be heard above the music. "Bring out more appetizers. *Empanadas*, a couple more shrimp cocktails, and stuffed avocados."

"Manny, where are we supposed to put all this food?" Talia teased.

He leaned forward with a twinkle in his eye. "The party's just getting started, *querida*."

Moments later, Manny pulled her from the chair, and with the group cheering her on, she stumbled through the salsa steps. Manny didn't allow his limp to limit him at all, and she laughed and covered her face when she stepped on the poor man's foot.

"Don't worry, you're doing fine," Manny said.

Tomas sat back and smiled, his gaze fixed on her so intently she blushed.

For the most part, the group refrained from speaking Spanish so she wouldn't be excluded from the conversations. That all changed when Bianca arrived. The fun and excitement Talia had cultivated with the others took a nosedive.

Tomas stood to greet her, and she rose on tiptoe to kiss him on the cheek. Her full bosom pressed into his chest and her lips landed close to his mouth.

"*¿Que bola, mami?*" He slipped an arm around her narrow waist to give her a one-armed hug.

The pretty Latina made her interest in Tomas, and that she didn't like having Talia around, obvious. She sat down on the other side of Tomas and leaned in close, laughing and touching his forearm, tossing her hair every so often. Talia gritted her teeth at the behavior, but what pushed her over the edge was how she spoke to Tomas in Spanish, and he responded in Spanish, so Talia couldn't participate in the conversation.

She rose abruptly from the table and walked into the dining room without saying a word, found the bathroom, and locked herself in. Only Maybeth ever made her feel insecure, but seeing someone make a play for Tomas right in front of her evoked the same feelings of inadequacy her grandmother regularly inspired. Months ago he'd denied sleeping with Bianca, but what about now? They hadn't made any promises to each other, and though she didn't think he was seeing anyone else, she hadn't asked.

And what had he and Talia been doing these past months, anyway? Didn't that count for something?

How long she stayed in there she didn't know, but when she exited, Tomas waited in the dimly lit hallway.

"Are you okay?" he asked, brow furrowed. "You've been in there a long time."

"Do you care?" Talia snapped, doing what she knew to do—defend, fight, deflect.

His head jerked back. "What's that supposed to mean?"

"What's that supposed to mean?" Talia repeated nastily. "You know damn well what I'm saying. Maybe we're not in an exclusive relationship, but you need to check Bianca."

"Check her?" The frown lines deepened.

"It means you should tell her to back the hell off," Talia said, placing her hands on her hips. "I don't care what you do when we're not together..." The untruth almost choked her coming out. "But you're here with me."

"Everybody knows we're here together, and Bianca is a friend. I told you that before."

"Maybe you see her as a friend." She poked his chest. "But she wants more, and she's being disrespectful. Talking to you in Spanish, touching all over you like you're her man. Maybe I should go out there and rub all over one of your friends and let him feel me up. How would you like that? You know what, maybe I'll do that right now, and let's see how you like it." She stared up at him, defiant. She'd gotten so worked up her breath came in short bursts.

His face transformed into a tight mask, and his jaw muscles worked as he fought some hidden emotion. "I understand," he said in a controlled voice that still managed to vibrate with displeasure. "You've made yourself very clear."

He pressed her back against the dark paneled wall. Scowling down at her, his light brown eyes became stormy and darkened. When he spoke, he enunciated each word. "And I never want to hear you imply, insinuate, or suggest another man is allowed to touch you again. We are establishing right here, right now, that this—us—we're exclusive. *¿Comprendes?*"

His mouth came down, hard and crushing, punctuating the words without giving her the chance to agree or disagree. He more or less branded her with the searing heat of his lips, one hand to the back of her head and the other around her waist so she couldn't move. Their tongues tangled in a heated, open-mouthed kiss.

Clutching the front of his shirt, Talia held on tight as he grabbed handfuls of her ass to pull her taut against him. Their hips grinded against each other, and even when a man cleared his throat and passed by on the way to the bathroom, they didn't stop the hot and heavy make out session.

When he lifted his head, her nipples were hard and she was shaking. He drew such strong emotions from her—anger, joy, passion. Always the extremes and no middle ground.

His own breathing was ragged and heavy. "*¿Comprendes?*" he repeated. His voice sounded like sandpaper had been dragged across his vocal chords.

"Yes." Talia lifted her fingers to her swollen, trembling lips. She'd learned her lesson. "I'll meet you outside. I need to go reapply my lipstick."

"Leave it. Let them see and know what we were doing." He outlined her mouth with the tip of his tongue and pressed his mouth firmly against hers again as a reminder he meant what he said.

Taking her hand, he led the way to the patio.

"We thought you had left," Manny said, a flicker of curiosity in his eyes. "But maybe you were busy." A smile of amusement hovered at the corners of his mouth, as if he had a pretty good idea what they'd been doing.

Tomas chuckled and Talia blushed. When they sat down, Bianca immediately started talking to him in Spanish again.

Tomas twisted his head in her direction. "Bianca, we need to speak in English because Talia doesn't speak Spanish."

"She doesn't?" Bianca cast a glance in Talia's direction. As if she really didn't know.

Fake bitch.

"*Lo siento*—I mean, I'm sorry," Bianca said.

Tomas rested his arm on the back of Talia's chair, sitting back with his legs spread wide so one knee touched hers. He started a conversation with one of the men across the table. Talia didn't know if he saw the malevolent look Bianca shot her, but nothing could spoil her good mood. Tomas had insisted they be exclusive.

She placed a hand on his muscular thigh, and he played in the short strands of hair at her nape, drawing circles with the tips of his fingers and sending tingles of pleasure down her spine. The lustful look he sent her warmed her in secret places and meant one thing only. When they went back to her place, she was going to get it.

Chapter Seventeen

Darkness had fallen hours ago, and Talia rushed out of the office after a long day. Starved, she couldn't wait to get home and eat a hearty meal. A week ago Tomas had made a delicious lasagna and she'd frozen half. Last night she removed the dish from the freezer with the intention of eating it for dinner tonight.

Tomas cooked like a chef and he made the best lasagna she'd ever tasted. He infused the dish with fresh basil and smothered the pasta in mozzarella. Thinking about the meal, her mouth watered on her way out the revolving door to the street.

When they didn't go out for dinner, he cooked for them. Arriving to the sight of him standing shirtless at the stove, fixing a meal of spaghetti and meatballs or soup and Cuban sandwiches was a powerful aphrodisiac. There was something so sexy about a man standing half naked at the stove, cooking from scratch. She never grew tired of the sight.

Outside she saw Carter on the sidewalk. She mumbled a good night, intending to walk by.

"Talia." Her surprise must have shown on her face because his lips twisted into a self-deprecating smile. "Do you think we could talk for a minute?"

"Sure," she agreed. They rarely spoke, except about work related topics, and right now, they weren't working on any projects together.

"I'll only take a minute of your time," he promised. He moved closer to the building, out of the way of other workers heading home for the evening. She followed. "I want to talk to you about the day of the housewarming party."

She'd almost forgotten about the confrontation at Shawna's. It had taken place months ago. "Oh."

"The things I said..." He grimaced. "I didn't mean them."

"Of course you did."

"No, I didn't. Did you mean what you said?"

She considered his question. She'd been angry and hurt at the party. She didn't hate Carter, but she'd said the cruelest things she could think of. "No, I was trying to hurt you," she admitted.

His shoulders relaxed. "That's what I figured. Because of Paula."

"You shouldn't have brought her to my friends' party," she said in a hard tone.

He raised his hands in surrender. "Agreed. I know you and Shawna are best friends, but I considered her my friend, too. In my defense, I really didn't think you'd be there. The idea was to get in and get out fast."

She cocked a brow in skepticism.

"Okay, maybe I wanted to show off a little bit," he admitted. "You were the one who asked for the divorce, and I guess...I hoped to show everyone how well I was doing. But we didn't plan to stay long." His eyes pleaded for understanding.

"It doesn't matter now, I suppose. It's water under the bridge, and hopefully we can move on. We were married for a long time and being apart took time to get used to."

"Took?" he repeated. "You're already used to it?"

Perhaps because they'd already grown apart by the time she asked him for a divorce, getting accustomed to living alone didn't take as long as she'd thought it would. "We lived in the same house but barely saw each other and weren't sleeping in the same bed anymore. Maybe if we had been I would have felt more of a loss."

He nodded, appreciative of her honesty. "We did have a good relationship for a while." The statement sounded like a question.

"We did," Talia agreed.

A thoughtful look entered his eyes. "You're different," he remarked.

"Am I?" Talia self-consciously touched her hair.

"Not physically. I don't know what it is. Happier, maybe?" He searched her face.

"Oh. I suppose." She didn't know how to respond. It would be unkind to mention the difference was as a result of the new man in her life.

"Yes, you're definitely different," he declared with a firm nod. "Happier in a way you weren't before. Because of him? That Tomas guy?"

Talia thought it best to keep the answer short. "That might have something to do with it."

A pained expression crossed his features. "I have to admit, I'm a little jealous."

Her lips parted in surprise at such a confession. "Carter..."

"Don't feel sorry for me."

The conversation had taken an unexpected turn. "I don't know what to say."

"Don't look at me like that. There's nothing to say." He shrugged.

"I did love you once." She wanted to make that clear.

When they'd met, she didn't have any friends and had always felt uneasy and out of place, as if she didn't fit anywhere. Making friends had been hard, especially when she couldn't go out with them because Maybeth demanded she focus on her education. It became easier to keep to herself and project an image of cool indifference.

Carter had impressed her right away. In awe of him and his intellect, she couldn't understand what a worldly man of thirty-three could possibly see in her.

"You loved me, but not the way you love him."

Talia's couldn't respond, jarred by his assertion when she hadn't openly admitted her feelings to herself. Were her feelings for Tomas so obvious?

Being with him excited her, and she carried a giddy lightheadedness throughout the day, every day, even at work. Just today Lillian remarked on how mellow she'd become, and she'd dismissed the comment. But Carter had zeroed in on the reason for the change.

He shrugged. "It's my own fault. I should have protected you more from Maybeth."

Talia shook her head vehemently. "That wasn't your job, and I can handle my grandmother."

"Can you?"

She straightened her spine. "Why are you questioning me?" she asked sharply.

Carter fixed her with a penetrating stare. "Have you told Maybeth about him?"

Her eyes darted away to the afternoon traffic. She wanted Maybeth out of her personal life and out of this relationship. She ignored the question. "Were you the one who told her we were divorced?"

"I ran into her at a cocktail party Paula and I attended together. I had no choice."

She'd been part of that world for years but hadn't attended any formal events in a long time. She suddenly realized she didn't miss the stuffy dinner parties and polite conversations with people who had no more interest in her than she had in them.

"So, have you told Maybeth about him?" Carter prodded.

Talia hugged her waist. "No," she said shortly. Mentioning Maybeth had spoiled the evening.

"Why not? You're not ashamed of him, are you?"

Her eyes snapped back to him. "Of course not!" She wasn't ashamed, but her grandmother wouldn't understand.

"You know, I always felt she had too much control over your life. Her interference made our marriage difficult at times, as if we had a third person in the relationship. I could have done more to be a buffer between you, I guess, but you, more than anyone, need to stand up to her."

Carter had never before expressed an opinion about her relationship with her grandmother. Talia hated the truth of his words, but Maybeth had helped her become the woman she was today. Her guidance all these years was the reason Talia had achieved such success. Not only was she the only woman on the executive team, she was the only member under thirty. Maybeth always pushed her to want more and work harder, even if her methods of motivation were unconventional.

A taxi pulled up to the curb.

"That's my ride. My car's in the shop." Carter hung back. "Maybe we could have lunch one day, you know, to talk. Sometimes..." He looked away and gave a little shrug. "Sometimes I miss talking to you. You always kept me on my toes."

Talia smiled at the unexpected compliment. "Lunch wouldn't be so bad," she agreed.

When he started walking away, she touched his arm. Part of her felt a little sad. You couldn't be with someone for ten years—eleven if you counted the year they'd dated—and not feel a sense of loss when they were no longer part of your world.

"Even though our marriage didn't work, I'm grateful for all you did for me. I know you think you could have done more, but in a way you saved me from my grandmother. If we hadn't gotten married, I don't know what would have happened to me. You helped me grow up, and I'll always love you for it." She moved toward him and hesitated because he pulled back. But then he opened his arms and pulled her into his embrace. She hugged him tight. "I want you to be happy," she whispered, and she meant it.

He pulled away and nodded, keeping his head down, and she could tell he couldn't speak for the emotion in the moment. Nostalgia and regret hung between them.

He took a deep breath to compose himself and when their eyes met, he grinned at her. "I want you to be happy, too," he said. He squeezed her arm.

With one last lingering look, they said good night and headed in opposite directions.

****

Talia stopped on the way home and picked up a side salad to add to the lasagna. She washed down the meal with flavored water and then prepared for bed, thinking about the conversation with Carter and how much her life had changed since the divorce. She couldn't argue with his assessment that she was happier. Tomas had brought about a change that could only be termed as monumental. She had new friends now and concentrated on simpler pursuits she had never participated in before.

Tomas had taught her how to roller skate, and

last week they'd joined a few other couples at the paintball field. Her team lost miserably, but she'd had so much fun. He was always introducing her to new activities because he knew she hadn't had the opportunity to indulge in pastimes purely for fun and not for political or financial gain.

Talia rolled over in the bed. The more she thought about Tomas the more she wanted to see him. They hadn't seen each other in days and she missed him.

He went to bed early during the week, but since tomorrow was Saturday, he'd still be awake. They hadn't talked in a few days because of her busy schedule, and he didn't text, which drove her nuts. He considered texting an unnecessary evil and an excuse for people to avoid speaking to each other. He absolutely forbade her to use her smartphone at dinner and wasn't above confiscating it if she tried to sneak a peek at social media streams or secretly send a text when she thought he wasn't looking.

She picked up the phone and called him, and he answered on the second ring.

"What are you up to?" she asked.

"Six inches."

She laughed, turning onto her back and feeling better already now that she'd heard his voice. "I'm serious."

"Me, too. If you keep talking in that voice, my *pinga* will only get longer."

She didn't need a translator to explain what *pinga* meant. "I called to say hi because we haven't talked in a few days."

"So you were lying awake thinking about me?"

"No."

"Of course you were."

She rolled her eyes even though he couldn't see her. "Such arrogance should be outlawed."

He chuckled. The warm, inviting sound of his laugh never failed to make her smile. "So why are you calling me so late? Is this a booty call?"

"If it is, will you come?" She tugged her bottom lip between her teeth.

"Yes, and I'll make you come, too."

She giggled like a schoolgirl, half burying her face in the pillow. Being with him was so much fun. Until now, she hadn't realized something had been missing from her life. "How long will it take you to get here?"

"Five minutes."

"I'm serious."

"Me, too. I just pulled into your complex."

Talia bolted to a sitting position and patted the scarf covering the blue and orange flexirods in her hair. "Please tell me you're kidding."

"I'm not. You wanted me, and I'll be there soon."

"I'll be waiting," she said, scrambling out of bed.

After they hung up, she ran to the bathroom and yanked the rods out of her hair, laughing to herself. If he saw her he'd make one of his generalized statements about women. Imparting his so-called knowledge from years of observation.

Women. You think too much. You're way more concerned about your hair than we are. Don't get me wrong, we like it, but we don't pay as much attention to it

*as you think. That's why so many men get into trouble
when they don't notice their woman's new hairstyle. Now
bigger breasts, that's something we'd notice.*

She ran her fingers through the curls until they
fell into place around her face. Maybe she
suffered from a bout of vanity, but she wasn't
ready for him to see her with curlers in her hair
yet.

She took a good look at herself and wondered
what was happening. Overly bright eyes, flushed
cheeks, and these feelings she had for him
bordered on dangerous. The level of excitement
that surged within her every time she heard his
voice or knew she'd have the chance to see him
were all so foreign. Tomas could hurt her way
more than the pain she'd felt a few months ago
when her marriage ended. Yet she continued on
this adventure with him because she couldn't
stop. She didn't know how to at this point.

She heard him coming up the stairs and
hustled out of the bathroom to slide under the
covers and tried to look natural. He walked in
and her heart made a giant leap in her throat. He
filled the room with his presence, moving
quietly—slow and sexy.

He undressed in the dark, and she rose up on
one elbow to watch him. "You're being rather
presumptuous, aren't you? No hello, and you just
start getting naked?"

"Hello."

She faked a yawn. "I'm going to sleep."

"No you're not. Not now that I'm here."

When he was completely nude, she welcomed
him onto the bed with open arms. He skated his

hand under her nightie, tracing the curve of her hip up to her waist. "Why aren't you naked?" he asked, sounding incredulous. "I told you I was coming."

"You're way too confident." She threaded her fingers through his hair and out of his face. He'd recently showered, the refreshing scent of bergamot and lime a welcomed aroma. "I'm going to have to find a way to humble you."

"You can try, but it won't happen." He kissed her lightly on the mouth. "One minute."

"Where are you going?"

He went over to her closet. Slivers of light from the street lamps outside illuminated his back and thighs. It should be illegal to be that breathtaking, to have a body so hard and defined it appeared to be carved from granite.

"What are you doing in there?" she asked.

He didn't reply, but he reappeared holding a pair of red heels by the straps. "I want you to wear these," he said.

He had a thing for her in heels—the higher the better. His eyes would darken as he watched her strip off every piece of clothing except her shoes. This was the first time he requested the red ones, but he liked her in that color. She'd bought extra pairs of matching bras and panties in red because he couldn't seem to control himself when he saw the bright hue against her dark coloring.

In the dim light, she saw the cocky grin on his face and knew if he asked her to dance on the highway in the middle of Atlanta's rush hour traffic she might do it just because he asked. She couldn't resist giving him anything he requested. Their relationship had come to that point.

Because I'm in love with him. Her stomach quivered at the scary thought.

How quickly and easily she'd fallen for him was unsettling. But she accepted the truth of her feelings, even though such depth of emotion made her a little afraid.

Sticking out one foot from under the sheet, Talia pointed her toes at him. "Put them on me," she said.

Chapter Eighteen

A pretty fall day in early autumn, Talia sat on the porch with her laptop while Tomas cut the grass on the riding lawn mower. Even with the Georgia heat at a more manageable level, he still had a thin layer of sweat on his muscular back as he rode around his large property with his earphones on, listening to the latest music on the local Latin radio station.

She'd grown to love the country as much as he did. Despite her complaints about the long drive, she preferred to stay out there instead of at her place. The peace and quiet kept her coming back, and the bugs weren't nearly as bad as she'd thought they would be. Citronella candles had become her best friends, and Tomas sprayed the bushes with repellant where the mosquitoes converged so they wouldn't disturb her.

He finished the grass and she watched him walk over to the porch, wiping his face with a washcloth, the gold necklace on his chest reflecting the sun's rays. He sat in the chair beside her, and she smelled the earth and musky sweat from him having been out in the sun for the greater part of the day.

He turned to her with concern in his eyes and rubbed her back. "How do you feel now?"

She hadn't been well the past couple of days. Yesterday morning a bout of nausea had attacked her on the way to work and she'd thrown up her breakfast. First thing this morning she'd vomited again almost as soon as she woke up. She'd made an appointment with her doctor for Monday because what she thought was a twenty-four hour bug had turned into a seventy-two hour nuisance. If she continued to feel ill, hopefully the doctor could tell her what was wrong.

"I'm better," she replied. "I ate all the soup and crackers." He'd put her back to bed after she'd thrown up and went to the store to get crackers and the ingredients for chicken soup. His Cuban version included fresh cilantro and chopped green onions.

"Good."

Silence descended between them and she could tell he had something else he wanted to say. She could almost hear the wheels turning in his head, but she didn't push. She continued to type notes into the computer while she waited him out.

"Since you're out here so much, you might as well leave a few things here. There's plenty of space in the bathroom, and I could move some clothes around so you could take one of the drawers."

Talia kept her eyes on the computer but no

longer saw the words on the screen. Surprise didn't adequately describe how she felt. Stunned was more like it. "That would definitely be convenient." Inside she turned cartwheels but outwardly kept her voice neutral.

Their gazes met and held, and in that moment she knew that this was not only a big step for him, it was a big step for *them*. They'd been seeing each other for almost five months, but she always packed her toiletries and clothes and took everything with her when she went back to her place after the weekend. She didn't even leave a toothbrush there, loathed to be accused of being one of those women who prematurely tried to mark her territory. They'd already had that conversation when she accidentally left the sunglasses. But this was a new phase in a relationship that so far had progressed with a speed neither of them could have anticipated.

"Then it's settled," he said, his expression inscrutable. Was he turning cartwheels on the inside, too, and hiding how important this move was to him? "When you come back next week bring extra clothes, shower gel, and all that other crap you're always hauling back and forth in your weekend bag. Just leave them here."

He playfully tugged a loose twist in her hair. Over the past couple of weeks she'd succumbed to her hairdresser's suggestion to stop flat-ironing her hair and experiment with wearing her natural coils in other styles. Today she wore a flat twist updo and he'd complimented her on the hairdo earlier. She really didn't think she could do any wrong where he was concerned.

"Sounds good. I will," she said lightly.

"I'm going to take a shower." He stood and stretched. The taut muscles of his chest and arms bunched in a display of male perfection. "Then I'm going back to the store. Tonight you learn to make black beans." The mood shifted to a lighter tone.

"Aw." She pouted, hoping to change his mind, but knowing she couldn't.

"No more avoiding. Beans and rice are the keys to a Cuban man's heart."

"I thought great sex was the key to a Cuban man's heart," she offered helpfully.

"That, too," he said, and then he hesitated. For long seconds they looked at each other. In the past she would have fidgeted and shied away from his scrutiny. Now she held his gaze, hopeful, knowing he wanted to say more but something held him back. Then he grinned and the moment was lost.

He went into the house and Talia thought about joining him in the shower but refrained, preferring to stay with her thoughts and let the gravity of what had transpired sink in. He was making space for her in his house, and they'd advanced to talking about hearts. A smile slowly spread across her face. She'd never thought she'd be ready for a relationship so soon after her marriage ended, but this one was working out nicely.

****

Upstairs, Tomas was in the process of doing something he never envisioned doing—shifting clothes from the top drawer of his bureau to make way for a woman's clothes. He hadn't even planned to make the suggestion to Talia, but it made perfect sense considering how much time she spent at the house with him.

Granted, his home was his sanctuary, and he'd never risked even hinting to another woman she should leave anything behind, not that it stopped them. Women could be as bad as men when marking their territory. They may start with leaving a toothbrush in your bathroom, only for the sake of convenience, they'd say. Then they'd leave one or two articles of clothing, so they'd have clothes to change into when they slept over.

Others were downright sneaky, leaving panties or bras stuffed in the sofa cushions or under a pillow, in the hope another woman would find it. When he found underwear—or the even harder to detect earrings—he generally tossed them because he never knew who they belonged to.

But Talia hadn't done any of that. Aside from the sunglasses, which he'd long ago accepted she'd told the truth about, she never left a single item behind when she went home. Not even a toothbrush. Every weekend she took over his bathroom with her lotions, makeup, and hair products, and every weekend she packed them all up and stuffed them in a bag with her clothes. Then she walked out the door as if she didn't plan to come back.

He should be glad she took all her crap, but it bugged him. The bathroom counters looked extra empty after she left, and a sense of unease he couldn't shake always remained in the pit of his stomach for a day or two afterward. As if their relationship was only temporary and had an expiration date.

How ironic was it that the reason he guarded his privacy and didn't allow women to leave items at his house, was the very reason he wanted Talia to leave her clothes there. To create some semblance of permanence and continuity.

In truth, he liked having her around. She made him feel content, even when she drove him crazy. The search for the next hot woman no longer interested him because he had a hot woman, and she satisfied him in every way.

Looking down at the stack of dress shirts he pulled from the bureau, he remembered the weekend Talia showed up at his house with shopping bags in hand. She'd gone to the mall and purchased ties and shirts for him and proudly showed him the items when she came over. At first he'd been flattered that a woman had gone to so much trouble and bought him clothes, but when he took a look at the receipt that had fallen out of one of the bags, he balked at the prices.

"Sixty dollars for a tie!" he'd exclaimed. "I could probably buy ten for the same price."

"They're silk and were on sale," she'd said. "And these are good quality." She rubbed the fabric between her fingers and sounded so reasonable her explanation almost made sense— except it didn't.

"Talia, this is ridiculous."

"No, it's not," she'd said, looking hurt and disappointed. "I liked them and thought you'd look nice in them."

And so he'd tried on one of the shirts and

looped a tie around his neck. She'd shown him how to tie a proper Windsor knot since he hadn't worn a tie since he attended his father's funeral at the age of nine, and at that time his mother had knotted it for him.

When he'd seen the pleased expression on her face, he'd figured what the hell. He didn't look bad. Maybe wearing a tie and nice shirt every now and again wouldn't be so terrible, and if it made her happy...

"All right, we'll keep them," he'd said.

She'd squealed and jumped on him and proceeded to loosen the tie and undo the buttons on the shirt.

Back in the present, Tomas set the shirts on the top shelf of the closet. Slowly but surely, his life was changing because of her, but at least these were small changes. Ones he could handle and control.

Chapter Nineteen

Pregnant!

Sitting on the sofa in the living room, Talia was no more comfortable with the word than when her doctor had used it hours before. Her primary care physician had recommended she make an appointment to see her gynecologist when he couldn't find anything wrong with her.

Dr. Mehta had fit her in early Wednesday afternoon, and she'd stared at her doctor as if the woman had lost her mind. "Impossible. I'm on birth control."

But she was pregnant. The ultrasound showed a seven-week-old baby growing inside of her.

She'd missed a Depo shot appointment, but she hadn't been concerned because she'd thought she was still in the safe zone. And even though she hadn't had a cycle, she still hadn't worried because when stressed or under a heavy workload, or even when she increased her level of exercise, she might miss her period over the course of a month or two.

In a reasonable voice meant to calm but which had the opposite effect, her gynecologist had explained. "Statistically you should have been fine since you had your shot within two weeks of the scheduled date, but the only true safe zone is to get your shot within the twelve week guidelines." Her eyes turned sympathetic. "And you know that no contraceptive is one hundred percent effective."

Now she found herself in a predicament she couldn't have imagined—single and with an unwanted pregnancy. She'd never had to take care of anyone else before, nor had she ever babysat or changed a diaper in her life. Carter had wanted children, but she hadn't been willing to give them to him. Her career had taken precedence for years, because her only concern had been climbing the corporate ladder—and making her grandmother proud.

When she and Carter divorced she'd seen it as a blessing they hadn't had kids. Not only did children complicate divorce, she couldn't imagine being responsible for another human being. Certainly not a helpless, tiny creature who would look to her for all its needs.

She placed her hand over her flat stomach, trying to imagine what it would be like to be someone's mother. How could she care for someone else?

She thought about all the changes Shawna had gone through after Ryker's birth. "Your priorities change," Shawna had told her once, as if that explained everything.

Ryker had taken over her friends' home. Once he'd started walking, every room had to be baby-proofed. Cushions protected against the sharp corners of furniture and each outlet had a plug covering it. Shawna and Ryan couldn't make plans unless they coordinated babysitting or at a minimum, where they were going accommodated children. She was tired just thinking of all the rearranging she'd have to do if she had a child.

Not if, but when.

Because if all went well with this pregnancy, despite the fear of raising another human being and the inevitable disruption to her life, she wanted to have this baby.

But what would Tomas think?

What would he say?

****

Talia decided to wait until she saw Tomas on Friday to tell him about her pregnancy in person. It gave her time to rehearse the lines in her head, but as the time drew nearer, she became more anxious. She'd left work earlier than usual, her stomach a tangle of nerves. They'd never said 'I love you,' but she didn't doubt he cared for her.

The doorbell rang while she packed a bag for the weekend, but she ignored it because Tomas had a key and would come right in. Chances were some group or another was soliciting and had ignored the No Solicitation sign at the front of the complex. They loved to come by, which was extremely annoying.

The doorbell rang again, two more times and more insistently. Exasperated, she ran downstairs, ready to give the person a piece of her mind. She yanked open the door and Maybeth's scowling face greeted her.

"You kept me waiting long enough." Her grandmother traipsed in wearing a pencil skirt, a green blouse, and a bouclé jacket with three-quarter length sleeves. The jasmine notes of Chanel No. 5 whisked in with her. Maybeth's sharp gaze swept her from head to toe. "My goodness, what is the matter with you? Do you need a new hairdresser? And what are you wearing?"

"I wasn't expecting you." Talia patted her hair, which Tomas had loved but Maybeth clearly saw as inappropriate.

Straightening her spine, she remembered all the reprimands she'd received as a child about the importance of good posture. She tugged on her oversized T-shirt—Tomas's actually—in a pointless attempt to hide the cut-off jeans she wore.

Maybeth sighed. "'I wasn't expecting you' is not an acceptable answer. One must always be prepared for company, Talia." She stood in the middle of the room with her purse hanging from the crook of an arm. Her critical eye assessed the condo. "Good heavens, what have you done to the place?"

Red passion paint covered the accent wall in the living room and one in the kitchen, and Talia had purchased furnishings and pillows in the same vibrant hue. In addition, Tomas had painted the bathrooms tan and forest green, and she'd bought a slew of towels and bathroom accessories to match.

"I've done a little redecorating," Talia said softly, suddenly regretful about changes that had brought her joy for months.

"Red is rather garish, don't you think?" Maybeth said, and Talia braced herself for more criticism. But to her surprise, her grandmother asked, "How are things?" A simple enough question, but it sounded loaded.

"Fine."

Maybeth went to the grouping of chairs in the living room and sat in the middle of the sofa. She crossed her legs. "I would like a glass of water if it's not too much to ask."

In the kitchen Talia gave herself a pep talk. She was a grown woman and the senior vice president of creative services at a successful marketing firm. She could handle this. An unexpected visit from Maybeth wouldn't throw her off.

The entire conversation in her head was all for naught, because when she handed the glass to Maybeth, she felt as small and insignificant as she always did. She wished she could make the feeling go away, but it remained unshakable.

"You're dating again." Maybeth took a sip of the water and placed the glass on the table in front of her. "When you're done staring like a deer in headlights, maybe you can tell me about him."

"I—"

"Have a seat." Maybeth gestured at the chair across from her.

Talia sat down and folded her hands in her lap. Tension tightened her shoulders and would leave her muscles sore after Maybeth left.

She caught the fault-finding look her grandmother gave her attire yet again. Maybeth didn't say a word, but she didn't have to. She insisted a lady should always be well-dressed, even at home, and her expression of distaste spoke volumes.

"You were saying?"

Talia swallowed. "Yes, I'm dating again."

"It wasn't a question, my dear, but a statement. I already know you're seeing someone, you see, because I overhead the cook telling the housekeeper she saw you leaving the supermarket hanging on the arm of a young man with long hair who—in her words—was absolutely delicious. So are you going to tell me about him, or do I need to hire a private investigator?"

Talia's fingers tightened in her lap. "He's..." Where to begin? How much to share?

"I see I'll have to lead with questions," Maybeth said, her face pinched and annoyed. "What does he do?"

"He's um..." Talia's voice shook and she paused to organize her thoughts. "He's a foreman. For a construction company."

"So he's a day laborer?"

"No, he's a foreman."

"How is that different?" Maybeth lifted a brow. "Never mind. What else?" She rolled her hand impatiently, an indication Talia should continue, but hurry.

"There's not much else to tell. I met him through mutual friends."

"Does he have a name?"

She hesitated, worried that telling Maybeth his name would somehow tear a gash in the shield she'd erected to protect the happiness she'd found. "Tomas Molina," she said quietly, reluctantly.

"You mean Thomas."

"No. Tomas."

"What kind of name is that?"

Talia swallowed. Dread building in her stomach. "He's Hispanic. From Cuba."

"That's different." Maybeth paused. "Is this serious?"

"We're..."

"*Speak up.*"

"No," Talia said quickly. "We're more friends than anything else."

That must have been the right answer because Maybeth gave her one of her smiles. A sight so rare Talia stared in amazement. The brief moment of acceptance softened the pang of guilt that nicked her conscience for not acknowledging her relationship with Tomas. She justified the untruth by reminding herself her grandmother wouldn't understand.

"Good. When you start dating again, you should date someone of your same ilk. Someone knowledgeable about the social graces and who can speak intellectually about politics and a variety of issues. Carter was a good start, but I was never completely satisfied with him. This Tomas person might be fine for someone else, but not for my granddaughter. Frankly, Talia, you should be more careful of these foreigners."

Maybeth stood and Talia did, too. "We need

to get you back out there, visible, so the right man can find you. You don't need a man, mind you, but it wouldn't hurt to meet someone with good connections—someone equally interested in upward mobility or the relationship won't work, and then you'd be better off alone. Sunday night I'm having a small soirée at my house for a couple of people running for state office. We're going to feel them out, get to know them before my friends and I offer financial support. I know it's short notice but I expect you to be there. Please do something with your hair.

"One of the candidates is a young man who might be right for you. Hard to say, but at least the right people will be there, so even if he's not, you're sure to rub elbows with someone who is. At any rate, this is only the beginning of many more of these events. Your social calendar will be full this fall. I'll be at quite a few gatherings where important people will be in attendance, and I expect you to accompany me. Oh, I almost forgot. How silly of me. There's another young man I want you to meet who will be at the party. His grandfather marched with Dr. King and was very influential in the Civil Rights Movement..."

Sickened with feelings of powerlessness, Talia shut down as Maybeth droned on. She couldn't hear her anymore. The walls closed in and reminded her of how her life used to be growing up, and even after she'd married Carter. Her grandmother had backed off somewhat once she married, but she'd still expected Talia, and her husband, to attend high profile events and network for Maybeth's causes.

Even in college, Maybeth had controlled every aspect of her life. Talia hadn't been allowed to live on campus. Instead, she stayed at home, missing out on the usual freshman activities. She used to eavesdrop on conversations, jealous as classmates bragged about their drinking binges, complained about having to share communal bathrooms, and joked about cramming for finals hours after coming in from frat parties and local clubs. She'd envied their freedom and longed for her own, only managing to gain some semblance of independence when she married Carter.

He'd become her rock and confidante. Maybeth grudgingly approved of him after a thorough background check and a sit-down conversation reminiscent of a job interview for the Secret Service. Their courtship graduated quickly to an engagement and then marriage.

"I'll have my assistant send you the details right away," Maybeth was saying.

"Okay." She'd learned a long time ago to simply agree and not say much. It made her life much easier.

They walked to the door, and Talia heard the key in the lock.

No!

Her belly quivered with fear. The one thing she didn't want, couldn't allow to happen because she simply wasn't ready, would take place in a few seconds and there was nothing she could do to stop it.

The door swung open and in walked Tomas, and he and Maybeth came face to face with each other.

Chapter Twenty

Tomas stared at the older woman next to Talia, right away guessing they must be related. The stylish clothes and similar features gave away the relationship. Silence reigned in the entryway as he and the woman examined each other, but he sent an inquisitive look in Talia's direction when the standoff stretched into an awkward length of time.

"This is Tomas," Talia said.

"Oh. The Cuban." She said it like he was a newly discovered species of animal. "I'm Maybeth Livingstone, Talia's grandmother. I'm sure she's told you all about me." So this was Talia's grandmother, the woman who with one phone call could spoil Talia's entire day and send her spiraling into semi-depression.

Tomas set down the plastic bag he brought in. He'd put off patching a couple of holes in the bathroom wall and Talia had said she wanted to paint her office. He intended to complete those small projects today and had stopped at the Home Depot to purchase spackling paste and paint.

Maybeth offered him her hand, and as he took it he searched Talia's face, silently willing her to tell him how to proceed with this woman, but her face gave him pause. She appeared...the word petrified came to mind. Her brow wrinkled into a frown of worry and he'd never seen such tension in her body before.

After two hard pumps of his hand, Maybeth glanced at the items he'd placed on the floor. "It's good to have a friend who's handy," she remarked. "And goodness knows she needs to do some work around here."

She looked him over and he wondered if the comment about needing to do work applied not only to the walls but him, as well. Her Royal Highness held her head at a haughty angle, and he had the sneaking suspicion he didn't meet her specifications.

"Well, I must be running. Talia, don't forget the party Sunday night."

"I won't."

After her grandmother left, Talia went into the living room and he followed. "Is everything all right?" he asked. He could tell it wasn't.

"Yes. Why do you ask?"

"You're off." No stranger to the swings her grandmother created in her moods, he knew she'd shut down like she always did, but he sensed she'd shut down even more than normal.

"I'm fine." She waved off his concern.

He stuffed his hands in his pockets, stared at the back of her head, and tried another tactic to get her to open up. "So, what party was she talking about?"

"Some silly political thing she's hosting at her house. It's nothing serious." She picked up a half-empty glass of water from the table in the living room. Oddly, she never turned in his direction once.

"But we're going?" He followed her into the kitchen where she set the glass in the sink.

"I'm going," she said, her voice sounding odd. "You're not. It's boring stuff. Boring political stuff."

"Maybe I want to go to a boring political party. Don't you need an escort?"

Talia turned from the kitchen sink and passed by him, continuing to avoid his eyes. "We'll see. I'm going upstairs to finish packing for the weekend."

He was no fool. He watched her run up the stairs and knew she was hiding something. Her answers didn't satisfy him, so he followed right after her.

"What does that mean? 'We'll see?'"

"Nothing." The flat tone concerned him.

"Why haven't I met your grandmother before?"

"No reason," she said. She sounded annoyed, which he couldn't understand. Why would his questions annoy her?

"She's a busy woman," Talia continued, walking to the closet. She still hadn't looked at him, probably the most disturbing part of the conversation. "She's always running here and there and everywhere."

The vague answer and tone of her voice sparked his curiosity. He trailed her into the bedroom closet.

"Let's go straight to your place, okay?" She finally lifted her gaze to him, and the overly bright smile didn't fool him. The desperate plea in her eyes increased his concern. "We can leave the painting for another time. I want to get out of here."

Tomas braced a hand on each side of the door. "Why haven't I met your grandmother before today? You've met all my friends and been to Manny's restaurant, attended my friend's daughter's *quinces* and other parties with me. You know my friends, but I don't know yours."

She pulled a shirt from the hanger and took a deep breath before turning to face him. "Don't do this, Tomas. It's not important."

Her answer didn't sit well with him. "What's not important?"

"We don't need to have this conversation. It's just a stupid party!" Her voice raised a full octave.

"Obviously this isn't a stupid party," he said quietly. "Why don't you want me to go?"

"It's not that I don't want you to go," she said, her voice sounding more conciliatory. "But you'll probably feel out of place and uncomfortable. It's one party, Tomas, and really not a big deal."

Anger simmered inside him. "You're lying to me. I want you to tell me the truth, and I want you to tell me now."

She ducked under his arm, and her body

brushed his as she slid out the door. "You don't want the truth."

Something he'd suspected, but never wanted to acknowledge, reared its ugly head. "You don't want me there."

She ignored his comment, unfolding and refolding the clothes in the bag.

"What are we doing, Talia?" He never yelled, but the more she ignored his questions, the louder his voice became. "Just having a good time? Is that all this is to you, and when you're done slumming it with me you'll go find another man who fits into your perfect little world?"

She swung around. "Stop it! You know I'm not like that. You know I'm not a snob."

"No?" He wanted to shake her, to force her to admit the truth. "Then why haven't I met your friends? We've been sleeping together for months now."

"You know I don't have a lot of friends."

He moved closer. "What about your grandmother? You didn't even want to introduce us a few minutes ago."

"You're being ridiculous."

"No, I'm not."

"You don't understand!" She covered her face.

"Make me understand." He refused to let up.

Her face transformed into a pain-filled mask. "I don't want to hurt you. Can we please not do this right now? Please, Tomas."

Her voice shook, but he had no pity for her. He felt as if someone had deposited a ton of lead in his stomach. "It's okay to sleep with me, but you don't want me at your fancy party. Is that it?

You think I don't know how to clean up? Are you ashamed of us? Worried I'll embarrass you?"

"No," she insisted, with a vehement shake of her head. "I don't even want to go to this stupid party. You don't understand what I have to deal with. You don't know what's it's like to be me."

"You're right, I don't. Because I'm not the one running around trying to be someone else and please another person instead of making myself happy. I learned long ago to be me. Being someone else is too much work."

He marched to the door.

"Where are you going?" she asked. "Don't go."

He paused, and when he turned to look at her, the stricken expression on her face made his gut clench. But he held firm. "Then let me go to your political party."

"It's not that simple." Her eyes begged him to understand. "My grandmother won't allow it. Give me a chance. Let me figure this out."

She was falling apart in front of his eyes, but instead of sympathizing, seeing her in such distress angered him. What the hell was wrong with her? Surely she understood the ridiculousness of her behavior, and how offensive she was being to him.

"What is there to figure out? You want me to wait around for you to make up your mind about whether or not I'm good enough?" He snorted. "Now I understand what your ex-husband meant when he yelled the warning to me at the housewarming party. But no need to worry. I'll leave so you can figure out what you want."

"I want you."

"No, you want this." He grabbed his crotch. "I told you before, I am more than my penis. I thought..."

With a frustrated shake of his head, he strode out of the room before he said something he regretted. Divulging his feelings would be a huge, embarrassing mistake when she'd made it clear she had no intention of acknowledging their relationship and he didn't fit into her world.

Talia chased him down the stairs. "Tomas, wait, please. Don't go. Let me figure this out." Hearing the quiver in her voice tore at him, but he gritted his teeth and resisted the urge to turn around and comfort her.

"*Tomas!*" His name tore from her throat, a desperate wail that sent goose bumps tearing across his shoulder blades.

He stopped a few feet from the front door. Turning slowly, he steeled his psyche, but he still wasn't prepared for the sight of her pretty brown eyes swimming in a pool of tears.

"Don't go," she said. "I'll do anything."

"No, you won't." Her grandmother had an unbreakable hold on her. "Go to your party, Talia." He walked to the door.

"You want to be this way, fine. If you leave, we are done. Do you understand me?" she screamed.

He paused with his hand on the doorknob and threw back his head, laughing. "An ultimatum? Did you really think that would work?"

A flicker of fear, and then her head tilted at an imperious angle, her small chin jutting out and nose in the air. "I'm not kidding."

"Ultimatums don't work on me," he explained. "And besides, what am I losing? Obviously, we don't have anything, right?"

He paused to let the words sink in, to let her think about what she was doing. If their relationship meant anything, now would be the time to speak up, but her silence was like a kick in the abdomen. She'd given him her answer. Everything they'd shared since the summer meant nothing.

What an idiot he'd become. At first, when she'd started spending the weekend at his place, every time she left his house to come back to the city, he told himself it was the last time, but the last time never came. He never grew tired of her.

Then he told himself the only reason they were together was because of the great sex, but the argument lost traction a long time ago, especially since he couldn't stomach the thought of another man touching her and had insisted they should be in a monogamous relationship. In fact, he'd stopped seeing other women long before he'd made his demand at Manny's.

Talia had made him think monogamy with the right person wasn't so bad and could actually work, and so he'd done a very foolish thing— something he'd avoided for all of his thirty-three years.

He'd fallen in love with her.

"Call me when you figure out what you want," he said.

He slammed the front door on the way out.

Chapter Twenty-one

Maybeth's small soirée turned out to be a semi-formal affair that included a handful of celebrities in addition to the politicians and her influential friends. Talia spent the evening avoiding her grandmother and smiling deferentially to the fifty or so guests, feigning interest in their conversations when she'd really rather be anywhere else but there.

The train of her stretched lace, sequined dress skimmed the carpet with each step. She'd chosen this outfit because not only did the design flatter her figure, the black color matched her morbid mood. Tomas hadn't contacted her, and she'd put off calling him. She'd seen the hurt in his eyes and her guilty conscience kept her from reaching out. She needed to give him enough time to calm down and not lance her with that accusatory look that gave her nightmares. Once he'd had a chance to cool off, she reasoned, he'd forgive her and realize she didn't mean what she'd said when she told him their relationship was over. She'd overreacted, panicked when she thought he'd been forcing her to choose between him or her grandmother.

And she still had to tell him about the baby.

So tonight she would dodge the aspiring politician and the grandson of the Civil Rights leader, whose names she couldn't even recall five minutes after she met them. And in another day or two, she'd give Tomas a call.

Maybeth spared no expense when she entertained, and tonight proved no different. Waiters moved inconspicuously around the room with canapés and wine, and Livingstone Manor practically sparkled. Talia hadn't been there to witness the transformation, but she knew her grandmother had gone over every corner and ledge with a white glove to ensure each room where guests would congregate had been buffed and polished to a high sheen. Even the antique Italian chandelier in the entryway appeared more brilliant than during her last visit.

Standing in the midst of the glitz and glamour, Talia examined her life. For as long as she could remember, every action she'd taken and decision she'd made had been for the sole purpose of pleasing her grandmother. Even tonight she'd shown up when she didn't want to, agreeing to entertain two men, sharp contrasts to the person she really wanted to be with.

She didn't belong there anymore, and she wasn't even sure she ever had. There was nothing wrong with this life except she didn't fit, and she worried about her child growing up under the same suffocating constraints she'd lived with all her life.

Maybeth had been right all along. She was more Jackson than Livingstone, and now all she longed for was the smell of fresh cut grass and the sound of the wind in the trees. And more than anything, her heart and body ached for the rough-hewn man who'd introduced her to this other way to live.

Talia spotted Maybeth near the hearth talking to a senator and walked over to her.

"Excuse me," she said. "May I interrupt for a moment?"

Her grandmother's lips tightened in displeasure, but rather than scold her, she nodded. The senator excused himself and made his way over to a small group of three a few feet away.

Feeling fearful but knowing she couldn't be the person her grandmother wanted her to be any longer, Talia clenched her fists to steady her rocky nerves. "I'm leaving, Grandmother."

An arched brow rose. "The party isn't over yet, and you certainly haven't spent enough time getting to know—"

"I'm not interested in either of those men."

Maybeth had always been the one to slice through her conversations. She'd never cut off her grandmother before. Not ever. Underneath the shock that she'd done such a thing, a sense of empowerment emerged. Her heart beat faster, but she recognized the rapid rate had nothing to do with fear.

Maybeth's face tightened into a forced smile. "You haven't given either of them a chance, dear," she said. She tilted the champagne flute to her lips and took a sip.

"And I won't be. The truth is, I..." This was it. She was strong. Capable. Maybeth looked bored with the conversation, but Talia pushed on. "The truth is, I don't want to be here. I don't want to meet anyone or be set up. I have someone, and...and he makes me happy."

"Is this about the Cuban? All right, you can have your little fling." Maybeth turned away, as if the conversation was over. She always ended the conversations, but not tonight.

"I don't need your permission," Talia said, loud enough that guests nearby abandoned their own conversations and paid closer attention.

The incredulous expression on Maybeth's face would have been comical under other circumstances.

"Talia Nicole," her grandmother said in a low, tight voice, "I do believe you have lost your damn mind." Her face still held a pleasant expression, but her eyes remained cool and hard. She didn't like scenes.

"I haven't lost my mind, but I've finally woken up. I want to be happy, and he makes me happy."

"My dear, he is not the right kind of man. Have your little fling and move on. Do you have any idea how the wrong man could destroy everything you've worked for? I will not let that happen to you."

All of a sudden Talia saw the vulnerable woman behind the haughty disdain. She'd heard rumors a long time ago, shared in confidence by family members who'd sworn her to secrecy, that her grandmother had been in love once, and had her heart broken. Maybeth never talked about her ex-husband, a man she married at a young age long before expanding her law practices into Alabama and Florida.

Someone getting the best of her grandmother was unimaginable. It must have been hard to love and lose and then decide those emotions weren't worth the potential heartache. As a defense, Maybeth must have closed herself off and concentrated on building her business.

"You blame yourself, don't you?" Talia whispered.

The room had fallen silent. The hum of whispering voices completely gone.

"What are you talking—"

"You blame yourself for my mother's death."

"Don't be ridiculous." Maybeth's shrill laugh filled the room. "Your mother—"

"You blame yourself, and you transferred your guilt onto me. You used your overbearing personality and guilt to keep me in line all these years, desperate not to lose me, too." Her voice grew thick with the grief of never knowing the woman who'd given her life and not being allowed to live the life she wanted to. "Because you needed me to be what my mother could have become if she hadn't made the choices she did. Was she unhappy with you, too? You can't force someone to be who you want them to be. My mother made her own decisions, and it had nothing to do with you. Her death was not my fault, and it wasn't yours, either."

"That's enough."

Maybeth slammed her glass atop the fireplace mantle. Her thin fingers sank into the tender flesh of Talia's upper arm, and she pulled her through the room, past the guests who'd turned into spectators. Outside in the hallway, she swung around.

"I have always protected you," she whispered fiercely. "I want you to live up to your full potential."

Driven and successful, she embodied everything Talia had aspired to be and everything she feared. She had always strived for the same level of success but realized now that though Maybeth had money and power, she lived in this big house with only servants to keep her company. That was the part Talia feared. Not finding anyone to love her the way she craved to be loved.

"How could I live up to my full potential with you constantly tearing me down?" Talia demanded. "What's the point of success if you're never satisfied? I run, and you say run faster. I jump and you say jump higher."

"To inspire you," Maybeth insisted. "You could be anything you want. Apply yourself and you'll have success. If you give up now—"

"You make me feel like I'm never good enough! And you never allowed me to live, Grandmother. You never allowed me to make mistakes, and every time I did, you cut me down."

"To make you try harder and make you stronger. It's called tough love, Talia. You meet a little bit of conflict and you collapse? Where is your strength? Where is your gumption? You have no idea what it's like to struggle—*real* struggle. *I* know what it's like to work five times as hard and be five times as good to receive even a fraction of the respect of my counterparts, and all because of my skin and my gender." Maybeth's voice quivered. She took a deep breath and collected herself. "And when I do succeed, I am told the only reason I've attained my goals is as a result of special treatment *because* of my race and my gender." She laughed bitterly. "My dear, you must learn to sacrifice and move forward and work hard and never, ever settle. I will not let you settle, Talia."

"I'm not settling. Didn't you hear me? I love Tomas." It was freeing to say that and no longer hide her feelings. "I love him," she said again, louder this time. She might as well tell her everything. "And I'm pregnant."

Maybeth staggered back and her face turned ash gray. "Pregnant?" She sounded appalled. "Are you going to keep it?"

"Yes."

"Talia, you have options."

"I've already chosen the right one for me." Talia touched her chest, her voice earnest and asking her grandmother to understand. "I want to keep my baby."

A glossy sheen of tears transformed Maybeth's eyes. "You're making a terrible, terrible mistake. My God, Talia, what are you thinking? You're throwing away your life. Do you think I invested all that money in your education, buying you the best clothes, sending you to etiquette classes, so you could throw away your future? You are better than this. What can this man do for you? This is history repeating itself."

Maybeth touched her hand to her forehead and closed her eyes. When she opened them, she appeared more resolute and her mouth set in a determined line. "I will not accept anything you've said tonight, and I forgive you for your outbursts and your unladylike behavior." She pointed at the doorway of the room they'd left. "Now march back into that room and be polite and gracious like I taught you to be. We will discuss the baby situation after the party." She took a deep breath, straightened her shoulders, and walked away.

"No." Who knew such a tiny word could be so empowering?

Maybeth turned around slowly. "I beg your pardon?"

"No," Talia said again, firmer. "I *am* strong, and I *do* have gumption. And I refuse to spend the rest of my life trying to please you and make you proud of me. I've had enough. Nothing I do is good enough because I'm not perfect. I'm Talia Jackson. I am *not* Talia Livingstone."

Sadness filled her grandmother's eyes. "You have so much potential and could go so far. You're making a mistake—throwing away your life."

Talia tilted up her chin. "I'm sorry you feel that way, but you're wrong. I'm leaving, Grandmother."

"If you leave, don't you dare contact me again,

because I do not know you. You are not the young woman I raised."

Pain spiked through Talia's heart. She hesitated. Had her mother heard the same words years ago? Her heart hurt for the steps she was about to take, but she didn't see any other choice.

"I hope you don't mean that," Talia said in a broken whisper. "Because you're always welcomed in my life."

Without looking back, she hurried down the hall to the front door and noticed what she thought was a smile of approval on the butler's face. He swung the door wide open as she approached.

Hitching up her dress so it wouldn't impede her steps by dragging on the ground, she hurried out. A rogue Cinderella escaping the ball.

She only hoped her prince could forgive her.

Chapter Twenty-two

"Talia, wait!"

Dressed in a black tux, Carter ran up beside her. She'd had no idea he'd been on the guest list, and she hadn't seen him inside. He must have just arrived.

"Where are you going?" he asked.

"You missed the excitement," Talia said ruefully.

"What happened?"

"My grandmother and I got into it."

His eyebrows lifted toward his hairline. "You and Maybeth?"

She nodded. He couldn't believe it anymore than she could. No one "got into it" with Maybeth Livingstone, but she'd never felt so free. As if finally unshackled from a heavy weight that had bogged her down for years.

"I'm leaving. She sent a car to pick me up tonight, so I'm going to call a taxi and go home. I can't do this with her anymore."

"Do what?"

"Everything. I want to be me and not someone else for a change."

"Wait a minute, you're not making sense."

"You were right. I should have stood up to her a long time ago. This was long overdue."

"If you have to leave, let me take you home. Besides, I'm dying to get the full story." His eyes filled with warmth. "Come on. The valet probably hasn't moved my car yet."

He took her by the elbow and escorted her to the far corner of the house. As suspected, the black Mercedes still sat near the front in a line of other vehicles. He retrieved his key from the young man nearby.

"Thanks for the ride," Talia said once they settled in. "You're going to miss the party, though."

"I'm sure I'm not missing much," Carter said, starting the car. "Anyway, I have to admit I can't wait to find out what happened between you and Maybeth."

"So you're not concerned about my well-being?" Talia teased.

"Oh, I am. But I—"

He never completed the sentence because the passenger door was yanked open with such force she couldn't believe it hadn't been torn off the hinges. Tomas glowered down at her. Big and powerful in pressed slacks, a black jacket, and striped tie. For a moment she could only gape at him. He looked like an avenging angel with his hair loose around his shoulders and his wheat-colored skin flushed an angry red to match his obvious mood. His eyes were shrouded with the shadows cast by the outdoor lights, but she could clearly see the curved lines of his mouth and the hard set of his jaw.

"Get out of the car."

"Tomas, what are you—"

"Get out of the car, Talia!" He didn't wait for her to move. One minute she was staring up at him, the next he had unbuckled her seatbelt. She only managed to sputter an indignant protest as he hauled her out of the plush interior.

The hand on her arm seared her skin and against her will, her heart started an erratic charge beneath her ribs.

"Hey!" Carter hopped out on his side and started around the vehicle. "Who do you think you are?"

Tomas pointed at him, keeping his fingers curled around Talia's upper arm. "Stay out of this." He hadn't raised his voice, but his eyes dared Carter to challenge him.

"Carter, it's okay."

"Talia, say the word and I'll get help. Or call the police." Carter pointedly held up his phone.

Tomas's expression became murderous, hostility rolling off him in waves. "¡*Cállate cabrón*!"

Talia didn't know what he'd said but knew with absolute certainty he hadn't invited Carter for tea. She tried to pull away, but Tomas's grip only tightened.

"Let me go," she muttered beneath her breath.

"What do you think you're doing?" he demanded.

She could see his eyes now. They didn't hold a

smidgeon of warmth, but swam with cool anger, further chilling her on this fall night.

"What do you care? You walked out on me..." Her breath caught, and she clamped her mouth shut so he wouldn't hear the tremor in her voice.

"You know why I walked out," he shot back. Because she'd hurt him. Because he thought her a fake.

"Then why are you here?"

"Because we're not done and you damn well know it. I don't care how many ultimatums you toss out. You're not getting rid of me that easily." His eyes challenged hers.

"Talia, what's going on? Do you need me?" Carter's face and voice expressed confusion. He wanted to help but couldn't follow the conversation.

"She doesn't need you," Tomas said in a biting voice, his tense body wound so tight he could pounce at any moment.

His arm slipped around her waist and he held her tight as if he thought Carter might try to steal her away from him. Despite the anger, being so close to him again was nothing short of heaven. The warmth from his body seeped into her bones and she softened like putty into the hard planes of his frame. But the muscles in his neck were drawn tight in anger and she almost reached up to smooth away the tension in his skin.

"How about you let her tell me she doesn't need me?" Carter said.

Tomas looked down at her. "Tell him."

"I'm fine, Carter."

"I don't like the way he's holding onto you. Are you sure you're okay with this guy?"

"He won't hurt me." Not physically. Emotionally was another matter altogether.

"Satisfied now?" Tomas asked.

"If you need me, you know how to reach me," Carter said to her.

She nodded, setting Tomas off. "She won't need you. She has me. Let's go," he said to her, seething with barely contained anger.

He weaved their fingers together and escorted her to his Dodge Charger parked far from the front of the house. They didn't speak the entire time, and he held onto her as if he thought she would bolt at any minute. She took two steps for every one of his, but he paid no attention to her struggle to keep up.

He let her into the car and she watched him round the front to the driver's side. The weariness in her bones signaled the past few days catching up on her, and she blinked rapidly to fight back the tears threatening to fall.

"Where are we going?" she asked.

The car cruised to the end of the driveway and Tomas pulled into traffic. "To your house, so we can talk." A muscle in his jaw tightened. "Are you pregnant?"

Talia gasped. "How did you find out?"

"I went by your place to see if I could catch you before the party because I wanted to talk some sense into you. I saw the ultrasound lying on your nightstand." She could barely see his face in the dark car when he turned his head to her.

"Are you pregnant, and am I the father, or is it your ex-husband?"

"Yes, I am pregnant, but how could you think Carter—"

"What I saw tonight makes me wonder. I didn't know you two were so cozy." A healthy dose of bitterness and anger dripped from his voice, and he gripped the steering wheel so hard she saw the whites of his knuckles. "Have you been seeing him all along? Did you take him to the party instead of me?"

"No! Absolutely not, to both questions. My grandmother invited him, and I was about to leave when he offered me a ride home. I have not been seeing him—at least not in the way you mean. We've had lunch a few times, but that's it. You have to believe me." She touched his arm and the bicep flexed. She withdrew, unsure what such a reaction meant. "You're the father. I swear, and I planned to tell you, but we argued and I didn't get a chance to."

He remained silent, and for a few miles, she only heard the sound of the motor and the swish of vehicles going by. He seemed to be turning everything over in his head. "Are you keeping our baby?"

Our baby. Hearing him say the words out loud created a surge of emotion. She loved him so much. She couldn't imagine anything more wonderful than having his baby. "Yes, I am."

His shoulders relaxed and he let out a long breath.

Talia hadn't known what to expect and certainly hadn't intended for him to find out this way. She'd pretty much decided if he didn't want to have anything to do with her and the baby, she'd be fine and handle the situation on her own. But Tomas obviously wanted this child, and his response surpassed her expectations. Despite her independence, despite the strong front she portrayed to him, knowing she didn't have to do this alone filled her with an overwhelming sense of relief.

He turned in her direction with an indecipherable expression on his face. "We have decisions to make. Together."

Chapter Twenty-three

Tomas pulled into a parking space outside of Talia's condo. She opened the door on the ground floor and without waiting to see if he followed, started up the stairs. Her ebony hair was gathered at the nape in a thick ball held in place with a diamond-studded clip. With the two-carat diamonds in her ears, she epitomized class in her figure-hugging dress. He watched the sway of her hips and round ass as he climbed behind her, angry at the way she made his body ache in unfettered desire even when she upset him.

He'd spent the past couple of days trying to figure out whether or not being with Talia was worth the headache, and he kept coming to the same conclusion. She was worth it. Worth getting dressed up to see if he could impress her surly grandmother. Worth sharing his life and the good and bad disruptions that came with having her in it. Worth fighting to hold onto her, even if she didn't think he fit into her world.

"Would you like anything to drink?" she asked.

"What do you have?"

He followed her across the thick white carpet. In the kitchen she held up a bottled water and a Corona. Careful not to touch her and lose what little control he possessed not to yank her into his arms and kiss her senseless, he took the beer—his favorite, which she'd gotten into the habit of keeping in the refrigerator for him.

"How far along are you?"

"Seven weeks."

She took a swig of the water and he gulped the beer.

"You should have told me right away."

She stared down into the bottle. "I know. But we had that argument and..." She shrugged.

Unspoken pain suspended in the air between them, but he didn't want to relive their last argument. He'd spent enough time brooding over what he should have said and should have done.

"We need to make some decisions," he said.

She walked over to the white sofa and slipped off one of his favorite pairs of her heels—a pair of black Alexander McQueen pointy-toed pumps with gold tips. He loved to see her dainty feet in those shoes, prancing around butt naked until he couldn't take any more torment and grabbed her.

She curled her bare feet under her.

"Did you hear me?" he asked.

"Yes." She averted her face.

He followed her to the sofa and sat beside her. "Look at me."

"I didn't mean for this to happen," she said in a soft voice.

"So how did it happen?"

"I messed up with my shots."

She hung her head and it took a moment for him to realize she was crying. Her small shoulders shook, and the trembling was even more painful to watch because of the quietness of her weeping.

He muttered an expletive and pulled her to him, her petite frame fitting perfectly into the crook of his arm. Always had fit since the first time he held her. She buried her face in his shoulder and drew a long quivering breath, fresh sobs rocking her.

Much as she drove him crazy, he couldn't imagine life without her. He rested his cheek against her thick hair and inhaled the rosemary and mint scent, reminding him of all the times he'd rolled over in bed and pulled her curvy body closer. At times he'd delayed changing the pillowcases so he wouldn't lose the scent of her in his bed.

She wiggled free and he reluctantly let her go. "Sorry," she mumbled, wiping her cheeks. She stood and walked away. Without turning around she said, "I'm going to change."

She went upstairs and Tomas dropped his head against the back of the sofa to stare up at the twenty-foot ceiling.

He was going to be a father.

Maybe the gravity of the situation hadn't sunk

in yet, but the thought didn't scare him at all. In fact, a sensation akin to joy—euphoria, even—filled him. He'd always been extra careful with the women he slept with, but his relationship with Talia had been different. He'd more or less lost his mind with her and become so comfortable that after the first night they'd never used protection again.

"*Padre,*" he said aloud, trying out the word to see how he liked the sound. A smile lifted the corners of his mouth. He derived the kind of exultant pleasure from the word he imagined could only be surpassed when he actually heard his son or daughter call him father.

By the time Talia returned, he'd finished the beer, removed the jacket and tie, and unbuttoned the top button of his shirt. Talia had changed into a pair of jeans and a pale pink blouse. Her face had been washed clean of makeup and her eyes gave no indication she'd been crying.

Typical Talia. Present an exterior of perfection even though she hurt inside.

"Are you all right?" he asked.

"Yes, why wouldn't I be?"

"You were crying. You're upset. You're emotional. You don't have to pretend."

"I'm not pretending. I'm fine." She held up a menu. "Are you hungry? I mean, if you aren't, that's okay. I was going to order some food."

"I could eat."

"The Jamaican place?"

"Sure. Oxtails and red beans and rice for me. Don't forget to order extra *plantanos*—"

"*Plantanos.*" They completed the sentence at

the same time. "I know." Talia went into the kitchen and picked up the phone.

She always teasingly corrected him, "It's plantains," and he would say *plantanos* so she would do it. It had become a joke between them that sometimes he'd purposely use Spanish words so she could correct his English, but she didn't this time. They'd shared numerous moments like that, inside jokes no one else understood, sometimes speaking in tones that provoked concern in others because they didn't understand the way he and Talia badgered each other was just their way.

While she ordered the food, he went into the bathroom and washed his hands, and when he came out she'd already put down the phone and sat on a chair. He lowered onto the sofa across from her.

"Are you ready to talk?" he asked.

"What do you want to know?"

"Why didn't you want me to meet your grandmother?"

He needed an answer to that question because it had caused the argument. If she couldn't acknowledge their relationship, what future did they have? And without a doubt, he knew he wanted a future with her, but he couldn't be sure she wanted one with him. For the first time in his life, his rock solid confidence had been shaken.

Deep in thought, Talia stared down at her fingers. "My grandmother and I have a complicated relationship. She raised me after both my parents died. You know my mother died giving birth to me and my father died a few days later. But I didn't tell you he died because he'd lost the love of his life, gone to a bar and gotten drunk. I think the Fates had a vendetta against us because he ran off the road and later died of complications from his injuries."

She drew air into her lungs with a sharp inhale. "My paternal grandmother couldn't take care of me, and even though Grandmother had disowned my mother after she became pregnant, she took me in and hired a live-in nanny to care for me. We have this weird relationship, where she makes me feel like crap, and I do everything I can to prove I'm not crap." She sighed. "She wouldn't have approved of you, Tomas, and that's why I never introduced you. Not because I was ashamed of you, but because I wanted to protect what we had from her. I knew she would try to kill it and I didn't feel strong enough to fight her. I always felt like I owed her and wanted to make her proud of me. And I wanted to be worth it."

"Worth it?" Tomas said quietly.

Talia hung her head and tears fell onto her cheeks. She sniffed and wiped them away. "For a long time I've felt guilty about my parents' deaths," she said, her voice wobbling uncontrollably. "I wanted to be successful and achieve great things so the choice my mother made, to have me, wouldn't be in vain. I felt I had to do something—anything—to prove I was worth...dying for."

He'd had no idea she suffered from such flawed reasoning. He ached to pull her into his arms and ease away the hurt, but before he could get a word out, she continued talking. She told him about the confrontation with her grandmother at the party, and when she finished her recap, she fell silent, eyes on him, waiting.

"You told her you love me?" Tomas asked quietly.

"Yes." Talia couldn't read his expression. She stopped breathing, hoping he'd forgive her and believe her.

"*Ven acá.*"

She needed no further urging. She jumped up from the chair onto his lap. Straddling him, she melted into his embrace and buried her face in his neck.

"I shouldn't have let you leave thinking I didn't want to be with you, because that's absolutely not true. I'm sorry I wasn't brave." Her voice was muffled from her lips being pressed to his skin.

She begged without begging, her arms tight around his neck. She'd been afraid she would never know this feeling again—to be wrapped tight in his arms and breathe the intoxicating mixture of citrus cologne and his natural male scent. To draw strength from him and know she was worthy, and beautiful, and warm—all the attributes she'd never been allowed to acknowledge until he came along and convinced her otherwise.

Tomas gently kissed her lips, sending delicious tingles through her. Content, she rubbed her nose against his and smiled.

"I love you, too," he said. He brushed a hand over hair and stared into her eyes. "Did you know?"

"I do now," she whispered. She ran a hand down the front of his shirt. "I can't believe you put on a jacket *and* tie. For me?"

"I remembered you'd met your ex-husband at a political party, so I couldn't let you go and meet some other man. I figured if I was going to compete, I had to look the part."

"Trust me, you have no competition, and I love you just the way you are."

"So I could have shown up at the party in a pair of jeans and a T-shirt?"

"Well…"

"I'm kidding." He chuckled. That laugh. His beautiful, beautiful laugh.

"Thank goodness."

Tomas sobered and cocked his head. "What about the situation with your grandmother, Talia? Do you think she meant what she said about cutting you out of her life?"

Her shoulders slumped. "My grandmother only says what she means. So the answer is yes. She meant what she said and won't change her mind."

"You never know. One day…"

Talia shook her head. Optimistic thoughts would only lead to disappointment. "No."

"I'll do whatever it takes to make you happy and take care of you and our baby." He clasped her face between his hands. "We're raising this child together, and no one else comes between us. Understand?"

She nodded. "No one," she agreed.

"And we're getting married."

Startled, Talia wrapped her fingers around

both of his wrists. "Tomas, we don't have to do that." Not that she didn't want to, but the last thing she wanted was for him to feel some type of obligation to marry her.

"I want my child to have my name." He spoke in a calm, firm voice. The tone he always used which meant he wouldn't accept counter arguments.

"Your name will be on the birth certificate."

"Okay," he said slowly, "I want you to have my name."

A pleasurable warmth seeped into her bones. "Hypothetically speaking, if we got married, I wouldn't take your name. You'd be lucky if I hyphenate mine."

He dropped his hands and stared at her in disbelief. "You're going to tack Molina to the end? Whenever I see those names, the second name looks like it's going to fall off."

"Well, that's what we're going to do. Be thankful I'm even marrying you."

A broad grin spread across his mouth. "Is that your way of saying yes?"

"Maybe," she said coyly. "You didn't exactly ask me the right way. Where's the ring? And you're supposed to get down on one knee and bring me flowers and there's supposed to be a big production."

"I don't do big productions. Are you going to marry me or not?"

She pouted and he pulled her in to kiss away the pout and rub her back. The small, circular motions soothed and sent shivers running the length of her spine. "Fine, yes," she said with fake reluctance against his mouth, as if there had been any other option. "I guess I'll marry you."

They kissed long and slow. When they finally came up for air, they laid on the sofa together with him curled around her back. They discussed their future and the coming baby and argued about which one of them would spoil him or her most and which one would be the better disciplinarian. He placed his hand on her belly and she laid her hand over his, as though they practiced for the day when they would feel their child moving inside her womb.

And long after their dinner arrived, they continued to discuss what the future would hold.

Chapter Twenty-four

Two days later they skipped work and spent the day at Tomas's house. Since arriving there, he'd been acting odd. He kept checking his watch and looking out the window. When Talia asked him what was wrong he said nothing, but she knew something was amiss.

The next thing she knew, he hustled her outside and told her to look up. Her wonderful fiancé had invested in a big production after all. An airplane had skywritten *Talia, will you marry me?*

Tears filled her eyes. "How much did that cost, you crazy man?"

"Too much, and you don't deserve it."

He pulled her into his arms and kissed the back of her neck. "Maybe you deserve it a little bit," he whispered. "I can't wait to spend the rest of my life with you."

"I can't wait, either," she whispered back.

****

The wedding and reception were simple but elegant affairs. A few invited guests joined them for a candlelight ceremony in the Venetian Room in the historic Hurt Building of downtown Atlanta. Talia chose the colors Tiffany blue and silver, and both she and Tomas had their best friends, Ryan and Shawna, stand with them. Talia had contacted her grandmother and asked her to come, but Maybeth wouldn't budge on her decision to cut Talia from her life—the only black mark on an otherwise beautiful night.

When Tomas slipped the gold band on her finger that matched the yellow baguette-cut diamond engagement ring, a crushing sense of love and fulfillment overwhelmed her. Seeing the love reflected in his eyes was more than she had expected in such a short period, and she shed plenty of tears as they recited their vows to each other.

Despite the broken relationship with her grandmother, the rest of Talia's life cruised along perfectly. She reached out to her father's side of the family, and they welcomed her as if she'd been gone on a long vacation and they were glad to see her return safely. At work she approached Jay about letting her telecommute a few times per week so she could spend more time at the house in the country.

To her surprise, Jay had been amenable to the idea. He suggested more staff members could take advantage of the perk and instructed Human Resources to work on a policy for flex schedules and telecommuting.

Although she moved into Tomas's house, they held onto her condo because of the convenient location. They couldn't decide whether or not to rent it out, and sometimes they stayed there during the week and walked to their favorite restaurants in the neighborhood when they didn't cook at home.

The Johnsons approved the beer ad campaign, and Lillian's idea for a daycare was accepted with few modifications. Although it wouldn't be ready in time for when Talia's baby was born, she planned to take advantage of the facility once the daycare was open and staffed.

****

Their baby arrived one spring day, two days before they expected him...

"Push!" the doctor said.

"Goddammit, I am pushing!" Talia flopped back on the hospital bed, droplets of sweat beaded on her forehead. "When do the drugs kick in?"

"In about fifteen minutes," the doctor assured her.

"I don't want to do this anymore," she whimpered. She reached for Tomas's hand. "I change my mind."

"It's too late," Tomas said. Her face was scrunched in agony, and he wished he could take the pain from her. "You're going to give me my son or I'll never forgive you."

"I hate you so much," she muttered.

He grinned. Just the reaction he needed her to have. That was his Talia. He lifted her hand to his lips.

She screamed from the pain of another contraction, squeezing his hand so tight he almost dropped to his knees.

"When do the drugs kick in?" he croaked.

An hour later, their son Manuel was born.

****

Tomas stood in the doorway of the hospital room watching Talia with their son.

"I finally got him to latch on to my breast and nurse," she said proudly, eyes glowing. Swaddled in a pale blue blanket, Manuel slept soundly now he had a full belly.

"Good." She'd worried quite a bit about breastfeeding when Manuel hadn't immediately taken her breast, and she'd listened carefully to the instructions from the nurse to make sure she did everything correctly. He knew how badly she wanted to be a good mother. She'd collected dozens of books and magazines on child rearing. She approached motherhood with the same focus and tenacity she did her career in advertising. "By the way, there's someone here to see you."

On cue, Maybeth swept in, chicly dressed in black slacks, a dark blouse, and a Versace scarf around her neck.

"I'm here to see my great-grandson."

Behind her, Tomas cleared his throat.

Maybeth tossed a glance over her shoulder at him and set her purse on the table beside the bed. "May I please see my great-grandson?"

Dazed, Talia handed over the baby to her grandmother, who settled into a chair beside the bed. Maybeth stared at him for a long time before her taut features transformed into soft lines and her chin wobbled. "He has your mother's nose," she said, her voice vibrating with emotion.

"You think so?"

"Yes. Definitely. That's Theresa's nose."

Talia's tear-filled eyes met Tomas's, and he saw the appreciation for what he'd done. "Thank you," she mouthed.

He left them alone and went out to the lobby as Ryan and Shawna stepped out of the elevator with a bouquet of flowers and balloons in hand. "How is she?" Shawna asked.

"Great. Her grandmother is in there now."

"Maybeth?" Shawna asked in a stricken voice.

Tomas chuckled. "Yes, but don't worry. She had a change of heart."

Thanks to a little prodding on his part. He'd gone to her office downtown wearing a tailored jacket and one of the shirts and silk ties Talia had bought him. He was shown into Maybeth's office and they'd had a nice long talk, at the end of which he'd backed her into the chair behind her desk. Resting his hands on the seat arms, he'd leaned over her. Her nostrils had quivered as she fought to remain defiant.

"I don't care what you think about me, that I'm Cuban, that I'm an average guy with an average job who's not good enough for your granddaughter. None of that matters to me because I will take care of my wife and my son, even if I have to work five jobs. They will never need anything as long as I have the ability to work. But I do care about how your behavior affects my family, and there are two things I will not let you do. I won't let you come between me and Talia, and I won't let you hurt her or our son." Then he'd straightened. "You have two choices. You can come with me and meet your great-grandson and help Talia, a new mother who could use the help. Or you can stay here and be miserable and miss out on getting to know our wonderful little boy. It's your choice."

Maybeth hadn't moved or spoken. She had laced him with a cold, deadly stare, using a tactic he imagined had worked on others. "Young man, no one speaks to me that way."

But she'd come with him.

"I'll go check on Talia," Shawna said now.

When she left, Tomas met Ryan's gaze. "So this is what it feels like," he said.

"Yeah."

Tomas chuckled. "Why didn't you tell me before, *amigo?*"

Epilogue

Tomas rolled over but didn't feel Talia beside him. The night before, she had opened the windows to let in the natural sounds of the country. Chirping crickets, crying Katydids, and frogs that lived near the lake's edge had created a chorus of sound that coaxed them to sleep like a lullaby. They couldn't do this in the summer because of the humidity. Now fall had arrived, with the overhead fan on low, the room remained the perfect temperature.

With his eyes still closed, he reached across the bed and touched her warm body wrapped in the red satin nightie he hadn't bothered to remove last night when he'd slipped inside of her.

"What are you doing all the way over there, *querida?*"

"Sorry," she mumbled.

He slid his arm under and around her and dragged her across the mattress until he could bury his face in her thick hair. The scent of her never failed to arouse him. He pulled the laced edge of the teddy up to her waist and hardened as he exposed her pantiless bottom. He lifted her hips into his and let out a low groan when her fleshy bottom made contact with his erection.

"That's why I was all the way over there," she said, but he heard the smile in her voice.

"There is no escape."

He cupped one breast and massaged the nipple with his thumb until she made the sexy little panting noises he liked to hear. Slipping his fingers between her legs, he found the wet heat that spurred him into action. Sliding his knee between her thighs, he slipped into her from behind. She gasped and reached back, curling her arm around his neck and arching her spine. He groaned as her internal muscles pulled him further into the warm, slick channel.

He took his time, letting his thick, hard flesh enjoy each sensuous stroke until she was begging him to hurry in a pained, breathless voice that threatened to sidetrack his self-control. He kissed her neck and ear, sucking on the tender lobe until her hand grabbed a handful of his hair. Close to coming, she tossed back her hips in a wild bucking motion.

Tomas held onto one breast and bound her to him with his arm. He watched as she parted her lips on a keening cry, eyes shut tight to manage the powerful orgasm that rolled through her. Only when he saw she'd been satisfied did he allow himself to let go. He gripped the mattress with his left hand in lieu of putting a strangle hold on her petite form as he endured a mighty climax of his own.

Afterward, she stretched, and he lay spent against her back, groaning into her hair.

"Mmm, good morning," she said, reaching back to stroke his bristled jaw with the back of her fingers.

"Good morning," he repeated with a low chuckle. As far as he was concerned, there was no better way to start the day.

****

Talia didn't know how long she slept, but when she awoke, Tomas stood at the window with Manuel in his arms. He wore only a pair of dark blue boxer briefs and spoke quietly to their son in Spanish. He was so good with Manuel. So many women had to barter with their husbands to assist with the parenting, but it wasn't an issue in their household.

She slipped from the bed and entered the adjoining bathroom, washed up and donned a robe before joining her two men at the window.

"How's my big boy today?"

She trailed her fingertips through the fine blonde hairs on Manuel's head. He observed her with his father's light brown eyes. She kissed his nose and was rewarded with a toothless grin. He was always well-behaved and had been a good baby inside the womb, too. Except for a couple weeks of morning sickness, her pregnancy had been uneventful. Even after he was born, he hadn't been too fussy. In fact, she'd worried about his placid demeanor and had taken him to the doctor. The pediatrician assured Talia that not all babies cried constantly, and so she accepted that he must have Tomas's temperament.

Sometimes she would stand over the crib and stare in awe at this tiny person who depended on her and marvel at her blessings, that she had such a good husband and a healthy baby.

She walked away, bare feet moving quietly on the carpeted floor. "What do you want for breakfast?" she asked.

"What do you feel like fixing?"

She paused with her hand on the doorjamb and turned to him. Big and brawny, framed by the sunlight pouring in through the window. Her husband, her lover, her friend.

She smiled. "How about some pancakes?"

The End

More Stories by Delaney Diamond

Hot Latin Men series
The Arrangement
Fight for Love
Private Acts
Second Chances
Hot Latin Men: Vol. I (print anthology)
Hot Latin Men: Vol. II (print anthology)

Hawthorne Family series
The Temptation of a Good Man
A Hard Man to Love
Here Comes Trouble
For Better or Worse
Hawthorne Family Series: Vol. I (print anthology)
Hawthorne Family Series: Vol. II (print anthology)

Love Unexpected series
The Blind Date
The Wrong Man

Bailar series (sweet/clean romance)
Worth Waiting For

Short Story
Subordinate Position
The Ultimate Merger

Free Stories
www.delaneydiamond.com

About the Author

Delaney Diamond is the bestselling author of sweet and sensual romance novels. Originally from the U.S. Virgin Islands, she now lives in Atlanta, Georgia. She has been an avid reader for as long as she can remember and in her spare time reads romance novels, mysteries, thrillers, and a fair amount of non-fiction.

When she's not busy reading or writing, she's in the kitchen trying out new recipes, dining at one of her favorite restaurants, or traveling to an interesting locale. She speaks fluent conversational French and can get by in Spanish. You can enjoy free reads and the first chapter of all her novels on her website.

Join her distribution list to get notices about new releases.

http://delaneydiamond.com
https://www.facebook.com/DelaneyDiamond

CPSIA information can be obtained at www.ICGtesting.com
Printed in the USA
LVOW13s1455130514

385604LV00001BA/12/P